I0621869

FIRST ENCOUNTER

THE SPECTRE wasn't as lucky. Since he was no longer hiding in the shadows, the Orderlies summoned by Dr. Hyneman spotted him before he even knew they were approaching. Granted, he was still just a silhouette before them in the darkened hallway, but he had been spotted.

"You there! Stop!" one of them shouted.

The two large Orderlies, used to wrestling with the insane, raced down the dark hallway towards him. Stuck in a dead end with no means of escape, The Spectre was forced to defend himself. He needn't have worried. Instinct and distant memories immediately took over. He moved without even thinking. His only fear was whether or not his body was up to the task.

He decked the first Orderly with a solid punch to the face, knocking him off balance. With a swift kick and a turn, he pinned the dazed man against the wall with a boot to the neck. Then let him drop to the floor, choking for air.

With lightning speed, The Spectre grabbed the second Orderly from behind and forced him to the floor with his arm twisted in a firm lock.

"Tell me where Miss Rose is!" The Black Spectre demanded.

The Orderly struggled against the dark figure's iron grip, his other arm flailing. There was no escape for him.

"Where is she?" The Spectre shouted, giving the Orderly's arm a quick jerk that cleanly snapped the bone. The defeated man gave a short whimper before answering.

ALSO BY THE AUTHOR

THE BLACK SPECTRE
Ghosts in the Asylum (Book I)
No Victory Without Scars (Book II)
Vengeance Waits at the Door (Book III)

Invitation to Death
and Other Exciting Adventures (Volume I)
Death is a Silent Intruder
and Other Exciting Adventures (Volume II)

For a complete list of books, visit:
www.blackhoodpress.com/all-books

THE BLACK SPECTRE

BOOK ONE

GHOSTS IN
THE ASYLUM

BLACK
HOOD
PRESS

THE BLACK SPECTRE:
GHOSTS IN THE ASYLUM
© 2012 Roger Alford

No portion of this publication may be reproduced or transmitted, in any form or by any means, without the express written permission of the copyright holder. Names, characters, places, and incidents featured in this publication either are the product of the author's imagination or used fictiously. Any resemblance to actual persons (living, dead, undead, or even mostly dead), events, institutions, or locales, without satiric intent, is coincidental.

Published by Black Hood Press
An imprint of Lightning Bug Press
5535 Robinhood Village Drive, #103
Winston-Salem, NC 27106

www.blackhoodpress.com

First Print Edition: June 2018
ISBN-10: 1-949352-00-5
ISBN-13: 978-1-949352-00-9

Printed in the United States of America

10 9 8 7 6 5 4 3 2 1

PROLOGUE

Terminal City, 1921.

THE two tough, young Soldatos drug Johnny Ricks by his collar into the cold waterfront warehouse as he struggled and kicked. Try as he might, there was no escape. Their grip was as tight as a lion's jaws clenched around the neck of a fallen gazelle. Choking out the last ounce of life in the desperate creature's body. Death was imminent. It was just a matter of time.

They threw Ricks to the floor. His chin struck the cold, rough concrete. Ricks wiped the blood from his face. He knew they would not be the last drops he would shed that night. While the rest of the city celebrated All Hallows' Eve, his only hope was that his voyage to join the dead would be painless, and that the Soldatos wouldn't torture him too much before they committed him to the grave.

A heavy pair of shiny, black and white shoes lumbered into view. Ricks didn't have to look up to know to whom they belonged. The impeccable white spats were a dead give-away. It was only a few seconds before the deep, husky voice that accompanied those shoes spoke up and confirmed the wearer's identity.

"Johnny Ricks."

The voice was filled with disgust. "Stand him up."

Before Ricks barely had time to react to the sound of his own name, the Soldatos scooped him up beneath his arms and propped him up on his feet. He couldn't have fallen if he'd wanted to. They held him firmly in place. They would control his every move until death provided the only escape.

"Big Jack" Torrisimo stepped out of the shadows. Dressed in white, he looked like the angel of death. His 14-carat pinky ring and matching tie pin had earned Torrisimo his other nickname: "Diamond Jack." Though it was heard less often, it was the one he much preferred. He was what the "Young Turks" (his American-born underlings) called a "Moustache Pete" — an old guard Mafioso who'd made his bones in the old country long before setting foot on American shores.

Big Jack grabbed Ricks by the collar, pulled him nose to nose and looked him dead in the eye. Big Jack was not a tall man, but he was certainly imposing. Ricks had no choice but to study Big Jack's features. Thick, coal black hair was slicked back across his large forehead. Bushy brows hid the deep-set eyes from the few lights overhead. The mouth was hidden by a thick, black, walrus moustache. The chin was covered with the dark shadow of a beard that refused to be shaven.

Unblinking, Big Jack spoke again. "I hear you been talking to the D.A."

Ricks quivered and shook, and for an insane moment thought that he could actually lie his way out of this. "Big Jack, no, of course not. I'd never do anything like that! You know me!" It was useless and he knew it. Worse still, Big Jack knew it too.

"I don't like Stoolies, and I don't like liars, neither," answered Big Jack, frustrated. "You could'a at least had the guts to tell me the truth."

That was it. The torture that Ricks had so desperately wanted to avoid was now a given. He had sealed his own fate. And now he'd made it even worse.

It was only a split second, but time had moved very slowly between that instant when Ricks saw Big Jack give the nod and he heard the cock of a revolver behind his head. The sound had barely enough time to register in his mind before the shot rang out and the blast ripped through the back of his leg.

This time they let him fall.

Ricks hit the pavement, cried out in searing pain, and reached for the burning wound. Yes, there was more blood. There would be more still.

Big Jack's final words to him were short and deliberate as he uttered them through smiling teeth. "Trick or treat."

Even if Ricks had understood the ultimate irony of dying on Halloween, he still wouldn't have appreciated it.

As he recoiled from the initial agony, Ricks opened his eyes. All he could see were the shoes of the Soldato who shot him; his bright white spats dotted with Ricks' crimson blood.

He heard big Jack's voice once more as his footsteps plodded heavily away. "That D.A. is getting to be a problem I'd just as soon not have to deal with any more."

Vito "Spats" Gennaro answered him, "I know just the man for the job." The other Soldato chuckled in agreement as he toyed with the brass buttons on his tweed vest.

Death would come many hours later for Johnny Ricks. As he suspected, it was slow, painful, and welcome when it finally arrived.

His body was never found.

THE CHILDREN ran through the well-to-do neighborhood of Lakeview Heights, the most exclusive in all of Terminal City. They dashed from door-to-door in their expensive Halloween costumes, each one custom-made by family tailors and seamstresses. Trailing one particular pack in his Old West Sheriff costume was young Brent Gregor, all of age ten. Brent was small for his age and could barely keep up with the older kids.

Being last didn't matter, though — he was having too much fun. Any other day he would be smartly dressed in creased short pants with his brown hair neatly parted and slicked with tonic. But on this night, Brent was allowed to run free and just be a kid, not "the son of the District Attorney," or "sole heir to the Gregor fortune," as he was often described.

Though the Gregor family was among the wealthiest and most influential in Terminal City, it mattered little to the other children. Most especially to Julius Kennelly II, the oldest of the group. Julius was a tall, tousle-haired blond boy of fourteen, who always led the charge, no matter what the activity. He was certainly too old to Trick or Treat, but he'd learned long ago that rules were meant for other children. Not him. The kids of Lakeview Heights had their own class system, and while Julius was at the top, Brent was clearly at the bottom.

Julius, clad in his Pirate costume, guided the group to the Patterson House — a large, old manor with an ornate porch that sat well off the street. The children knew this house well, and it was a ritual for them to visit it each Halloween. For Brent and two other children his age, this was their first time. As part of this annual rite of passage, Julius spun the tale of why such a grand house in the wealthiest part of town had stood empty for well over ten years.

Brent stared up at the dark gables and iron railings that trimmed each corner of the roof. Even during the day the house was imposing. At night, it was downright frightening.

"It was one night, a long time ago," Julius began, using his pirate sword like a baton for greater effect. The children stood spellbound. "The father was away and the house caught fire with the mother and children trapped inside." Even for those who'd heard it many times before, the tale enraptured them just as much as when they'd heard it the first time.

"The inside of the house went up in a huge blaze! The firemen got here as quick as they could! They crashed through the door and just barely got back out with the kids, but when they tried to go back in and find the mother, it was too late. The flames were too great!" Julius swung his sword again.

"The fireman did the best they could to put out the blaze. The only things left standing were the outside walls and the chimney. The house was just an empty, charred shell."

Julius paced back and forth, letting the tension build. "And when everyone came out to look at the charred remains the next morning, they found the mother's body burned to pieces. And you know where she was?" Julius asked as he stared them all down.

A few of the kids shook their heads silently, while the rest just stared back, unable to answer.

"She was right there at the front door, trying to claw her way out!"

A shiver ran through the crowd.

Young Brent swallowed hard, ready to race home to the comfort of his own family. But he dared not move. He was just too frightened.

Julius continued. "When the father returned home, he was heartbroken. He had the house rebuilt, but he was too sad to live there and decided to move away. So he sold the house to a young man and his wife. But the house was haunted by the dead mother! Every night they could hear her screaming, clawing at the front door!"

The older children could barely contain themselves. They didn't know what was more frightening — the story itself or what they knew was to come next.

Julius glared down at them again. "So they sold the house, too. And the next family had the same thing happen to them. And the family after that. And the family after that! Every night, screaming and clawing! Screaming and clawing!"

Julius stood silent to let the fear sink into his young charges. It worked like a charm.

"That's why no one has lived there in over ten years. That's why the most expensive house in this whole neighborhood just sits here. Empty."

This was it. This was the cue to the older children to steel whatever nerves they had. The three younger children, Brent included, had no idea what was about to come.

"They say, if you go up on the porch at night and stare inside, you can see the mother's ghost, her body on fire, screaming and calling for help!"

Julius looked at them, eye to eye, one at a time. Pointing at each one with his sword, he asked, "So, who's brave enough to go up there and look?"

Brent immediately knew that he wasn't. He stepped quickly back behind the others so as not to be noticed. He hoped deep in his heart that someone else would decline, too, so that he would not be the only one.

Julius was the first to peer inside, of course, as he showed himself to be the bravest. One by one the other children followed and peered into the dark windows of the front door. Brent assumed that none of them saw anything, because they all turned away, giggling nervously. Still, that wasn't enough to give him courage enough to do it himself.

His heart sank as the other two young children, Billy Wentworth and his little sister Abigail, perhaps more afraid of Julius than whatever ghost lurked inside that old house, stepped up on the porch and gazed in as well.

At last, it was down to just him. He hoped that no one had noticed that he was the only one who had yet to take a turn.

But they did.

"Well?" Julius asked him, tapping his sword in his hand. "You gonna do it or not?"

Brent wanted nothing more than to race down the street, back to where Bernard Worthington, the family manservant, waited for him by the car. He stared wide-eyed back at Julius. His pulse pounded. His lip quivered. The other kids stared at him, too, waiting. If he chickened out, he'd never hear the end of it.

"Come on, you little baby!" shouted Julius. "Get up there!"

Brent stood frozen in fear. He wanted to move. He wanted to do something. But he did not want to go up on that porch.

He looked around for sympathy.

There was none.

"Come on, let's leave the little baby by himself," laughed Julius. "He needs to go home to his Mommy."

Julius started off, leading the other kids away.

"Wait!" called Brent.

Julius turned back around. This was Brent's final chance.

He looked up at the porch. He did everything he could to steel his courage and started down the walk. He gripped the tiny handles of his toy pistols. He knew they wouldn't do any good, but it still made him feel better. He could barely feel his feet touch the cold sidewalk before he found himself taking the first step of the creaking old porch.

Before him, inescapable, was the large front door. The bottom half was solid wood, but the top half was split into two large windows of equal size. There would be no quick peek. He would have to look deep inside.

Brent finally reached the door itself. There was just enough light from the gas street lamps to see into the front hallway. The inside was dark and littered with shadows. It still frightened him, but not so much as he had expected. He'd done it.

Brent felt a quick sense of relief and was just about to turn away when something caught his eye. It was glowing and just appeared out of the darkness.

Without thinking, he turned back to get a better look.

It was a face. A woman's face. She was in pain. He could have sworn she called out to him. "Help me!"

With ghostly hands, she clawed for the doorway.

Brent screamed at the top of his lungs and raced off the porch. He barreled straight through the gaggle of children, knocking some of them down in his wake.

He could hear Julius' laughter as he raced down the street as fast as his small legs could carry him. He didn't know if he'd truly seen a ghost or if it had only been his imagination. But he knew he wouldn't feel safe until he was home.

Brent rounded the corner and felt a huge sigh of relief when he saw Worthington standing next to the long, black family car. He ran straight into the portly Englishman's arms with such force that it nearly winded the middle-aged man. Worthington was a large teddy-bear of a fellow. His graying hair was combed back and neatly trimmed. His bushy beard and small wire-framed glasses complimented his gentle appearance.

Worthington looked down at his young charge, whose eyes were full of tears and whose body shook uncontrollably. Brent hugged him both for safety and because Worthington would only be employed with their family for another week. He'd known Worthington his whole life and just couldn't understand why the man was leaving. He didn't want to let go.

"Why, Master Gregor," Worthington asked in his warm, melodic voice. "Whatever is the matter?"

Brent just shivered and held him tightly.

As Worthington opened the car door, he looked up to see Julius and the other children round the corner, laughing.

Worthington reassured Brent as he ushered him inside, letting him sit up front with him. "In the car, Master Gregor, it's quite all right."

Worthington gave Julius and the others a stern look as he climbed behind the wheel and drove off.

Brent managed to calm down quite a bit on the short drive home. Though he was still shaken when they arrived, he was comforted by the sight of the Gregor mansion. It was a large, welcoming manor with expansive rolling greens. No place in the world made him feel safer.

Worthington pulled the large car to a stop in the grand, circular driveway. Brent finally spoke up and asked the same question he'd asked many times over for the past several weeks.

"Why are you moving away, Worthington?"

The stout gentleman sat quietly for a moment then attempted to explain once again. "It's not that I want to leave, Master Gregor, but my family lives back in England. I haven't seen them in a many years, and I just think it's time that I returned home." It was close enough to the truth that he thought Brent might understand. "If you went away for a long time, wouldn't you want to come back here? To be with your mother and father again?"

"Yes," Brent nodded tearfully.

"Well, then," Worthington continued, "that is why I must go home. To see my family again."

"Will you come visit us?" Brent asked.

"Why, yes, of course!" Worthington reassured him. "And you are most welcome to come and visit me. Any time you wish."

As Worthington led Brent through the great front doors into the grand foyer with its high, arched ceilings, he explained quietly to the other servants why they were home so early. The dark wood beams and tall ceilings always made Brent feel as if he were entering an impenetrable fortress.

Brent felt another sense of relief as he looked at the gleaming suit of armor, fitted with sword and mace that stood like a sentry in the hall. He always thought it protected him from any spirits, evil or otherwise. He really needed its protection that night.

Nanny Miriam rushed quickly in to lead Brent up the grand marble staircase that led to the second floor. Brent's young mother, Sarah, rushed up to her son's room, kissed his forehead and held him tightly until he had fully calmed down and was ready for his bath. Brent's mother was as beautiful as she was loving. He reached up to touch her soft auburn hair, which she'd already let down for the night to cascade across her shoulders.

After Miriam had gotten him ready for bed, Brent hoped that his father would be home soon. Though he was safely at home and recovered from his ordeal, he wouldn't feel truly comforted until his father was there with him.

BRENT sat up in bed the moment he heard his father come up the long, winding staircase and then down the hall. He knew his father's footsteps — quick and deliberate. Thomas Gregor was not a man who wasted time getting to where he was going. He was young and handsome, a man of courage and action. Everything a young son could dream his father to be.

Though it was very late, Brent had resisted falling asleep before his father returned from work at the Court House. Brent's eyes lit up when Thomas opened the door. He was tired, but smiling, happy to finally be home with his family.

"Did you win your case to-day, Father?" asked Brent.

"What are you still doing up?" Thomas asked, trying unsuccessfully to sound disappointed. His relief to be home, in the comfortable arms of his family, was too great for him to sound truly stern at this hour.

"He just couldn't get to sleep before you got home," Sarah Gregor's soft, soothing voice chimed in behind his father. "He had a bit of a fright to-night." Thomas brushed her tresses aside and gave her a soft kiss before going to Brent's bedside.

"Did you go with those kids to look at that old house?"

Brent looked down, answering, "Yes, Father."

Thomas shook his head, but he more than understood

the power of peer pressure. "It was that Julius Kennelly, wasn't it?" his father asked.

Brent hung his head again. "Yes, Father."

"Listen, Son," Thomas told him. "Being brave doesn't mean doing a dare just because some older child like Julius puts you up to it. Being brave is standing up for yourself. Not letting others push you around. Do you understand?"

"Yes, Father," Brent answered.

"Well, I hope it didn't frighten you too much."

"I saw something there, Father," Brent told him.

"Oh?" Thomas asked. Sarah perked up as well. She hadn't heard this part of the story.

"It was a face. A ghost. She cried out," Brent told him.

"Are you sure it wasn't just your imagination?" Thomas asked, unconvinced.

"I don't think so. It looked real." Whether it was real or not, Brent was certainly convinced.

"I assure you, Son, there's no such thing as ghosts. Now you need to go to sleep." Thomas kissed his young son on the forehead then tucked him beneath the wool covers. "You can tell me more about it to-morrow. I love you, Son."

"I love you, too, Father." Brent smiled. This is what he'd been waiting for. Now he could sleep soundly, comfortable and secure. Father was home.

As Thomas stood at the door, he held Sarah and looked proudly at his only child. Brent's young voice called out to him again.

"Father, are there any ghosts in our house? I hear noises at night."

Thomas and Sarah smiled, then he answered reassuringly, "I don't think so, but it's an old house, and if there are any ghosts, then they would all be family and they would be here to look over you, just the same as we all do."

Brent wished his parents good night then closed his eyes as his father pulled the door closed. "Not all the way, Father."

"Of course not," Thomas replied. He stopped so that a narrow bar of light from the hall stretched safely across the floor to Brent's bed on the opposite wall.

"I love you, Brent. Good-night."

SADLY, what Thomas and Sarah Gregor did not know is that there was a ghost out that night. A frightening one. While they were upstairs to tuck in Brent, they didn't suspect that the ghost was making his way through the darkness across the mansion grounds. Neither they, nor their servants — who had all retired for the night — heard the breaking of glass in a distant, downstairs room as the ghost made his way inside. They didn't sense the lumbering footsteps as the ghost wandered through the endless hallways to where a light shone down from the staircase.

They had no idea he was there at all until they came downstairs and he surprised them in the hallway. Sarah barely managed a scream before a large hand with only three fingers covered her mouth. The other pressed the muzzle of a gun to her head.

Thomas had no time to react, even if there were anything he could have done, before the husky voice barked out to him in broken English, "In there — if you wants her to live!"

"Three-Finger Ned" Vogel shoved Sarah forward, pointing them both towards Thomas' study. Moving into the dimly lit room filled with bookcases that stretched to the ceiling, Thomas was finally able to get a look at their attacker and assess the situation. Vogel towered over him and held his wife's very life in his iron grip. He was a huge man with bulldog-like features, dressed in a dark coat that seemed to barely contain his bulky form. There was nothing Thomas could do at the moment except comply and pray for her safety.

"Open the safe." Three-Finger Ned's instructions were quick and guttural. Thomas took one look in his wife's frightened eyes and wasted no time in doing exactly as Ned ordered. He pushed aside the framed portrait that covered the safe and spun the dial as fast as he could. In seconds, the vault was open. He looked back at Ned, hoping to be rewarded for his obedience.

"Empty it," was the only response.

Thomas looked frantically on the desk. He grabbed an empty portfolio from beside a sword-shaped letter opener and scooped the papers and money inside with one quick motion. He turned back to Ned again, pleading with his eyes for his wife's safe release. If only he'd had a weapon or some means to fight back. If anything were to happen to her or Brent, he thought, he would never forgive himself. Thank goodness Brent was upstairs asleep. Hopefully, he would stay safe.

BUT Brent wasn't asleep. He had nearly drifted off when he was jolted awake by his mother's stifled scream. He'd already faced one terror this night, but that one was nothing compared to what was happening now. Whether the previous ghost was real or imaginary, he had no idea. But this one was most definitely real.

Worried and frightened of what could be happening below, he crept to the top of the stairs just in time to see Ned force his parents into the study. Though he only caught a glimpse, it was certainly long enough to see the gun in Ned's hand.

They needed help. And there was no one there but him.

Brent ran quietly back to his parent's bedroom and pushed open the large door. It creaked just a bit — enough to make him stop and wait. But no additional sounds followed. As best he could tell, he was still safe.

He rushed to the phone. He didn't know how to call the police, but he knew well enough to ask for the Operator when he picked it up.

"Operator? Operator?" he whispered quietly, his voice full of panic.

There was no answer. The phone line was dead.

His young heart raced, terrified and barely able to think. Worthington and the other servants were all downstairs in the far wing. There was no way to reach them. If anything were to be done, Brent would have to act alone.

BERNARD WORTHINGTON sat quietly on the bed in his small, comfortable room. Being just off the kitchen at the far end of the wing, he was a bit removed from the main area of the house and generally out of earshot. For that reason, he spent little time there except for when he needed solitude. And for that purpose, his room was perfect. It was also why he had no idea what was going on at the other end of the great mansion.

His eyes wandered back and forth from the tiny crucifix that hung on the wall to the ceramic figurine of Mother Mary that sat on his dresser. Though he was still a deeply religious man, he knew that he'd been running from the Church, and his past, for far too long. As much as he hated to leave the Gregor family and particularly young Brent, whom he regarded as something of a son, he knew it was time to face up to that which he'd so desperately tried to escape. He should have known better. Though unlike Noah, his own personal whale had been welcoming, inviting, and familial. And that had made it so much harder to return to eyes of God and whatever judgment that entailed.

Looking back to Mother Mary, he crossed himself and said a short prayer for young Brent's continued safety. The boy's parents were two of the finest people Worthington had ever met. With Thomas Gregor's guidance, young Brent would grow up to be a fine man indeed. Worthington sincerely hoped that what he had told the lad earlier in the evening was true: that one day he *would* return. It was a promise that he certainly hoped to keep.

BRENT rushed back to the top of the stairs. He could hear the shouts of Ned and his father, broken only by his mother's cries.

As Brent gripped the dark wooden uprights of the banister, quivering from the sounds below, the words that his father had spoken just a short while ago suddenly came back to him. "Being brave is standing up for yourself. Not letting others push you around."

The man had a gun. That's why Brent's father couldn't fight back. But Brent had something his father didn't. He had surprise. He had to be brave. He had to do something to help. If he could knock away the man's gun, his father could fight.

Swallowing hard and mustering far more courage than he'd done to step on that porch, Brent crept quietly down the stairs.

Careful not to be seen, he slid silently to the suit of armor and quietly plucked the sword away from its mount. It was much easier to free than he expected and he almost dropped it.

Quickly, he moved to the open door of his father's study and peered inside. Just a few steps away, Ned stood there clutching his mother while his father bundled papers and valuables into a portfolio. Once again, fear overtook him. He was ready to drop the sword and run. But his father's words rang ceaselessly in his head. "Being brave is standing up for yourself."

With no more time to think, Brent made one bold move. Raising the heavy blade above his head, he charged in as fast as he could. He swung the sword down onto Ned's outstretched arm with the pistol. But the blade was old and it was dull, and it only managed to knock Ned's hand down, the pistol still in his grip. Ned shouted more in surprise than pain.

Sarah Gregor dropped to the floor as Ned whipped around to face his assailant. Ned had already pulled the trigger before Brent's young face registered in his mind. Both Thomas and Sarah's cries were immediately drowned out by the sound of the gun blast. Brent didn't even realize what was happening until the bullet ripped into his side and knocked him to the floor, stunned and bleeding.

In the only moment available to him, Thomas Gregor grabbed the letter opener from the desk and lunged at Ned's throat with all his might. But Ned was a formidable opponent and his deadly instincts were sharp and well-trained.

The second shot hit Thomas clean in the chest. He fell almost in mid-air and slumped down face first on the desk.

Instinct took over again as Ned pointed the gun once more at Sarah as she screamed and clambered for her husband. Without even thinking, he fired the gun a third time. The bullet threw her backwards as it grazed across her head. She crumpled to the floor in a hysteric bundle of tears, blood running down her beautiful, delicate face. Ned stared at her coldly, his large finger still on the trigger, taking in the realization of what he'd just done. He'd never killed a woman before.

Or a child, for that matter.

He hesitated, then lowered his pistol just a bit. Instinct told him that the threat was over. This had not gone at all as planned and there would be hell to pay.

He scooped up the portfolio from the floor, then leaned over Thomas Gregor's lifeless body. "This is what you get for sticking your nose where it don't belong."

Ned turned back to the door. Brent was lying there in a pool of blood, grasping his side. His face was turning pale. Approaching footsteps echoed down the distant hall. Maybe the kid would live, he thought. But if Ned didn't move soon, there would be still more killing to be done.

Ned returned to the prostrate corpse of Thomas Gregor. Young Brent watched in delirious confusion as Ned dipped a thick, stubby finger into his father's blood and drew an "X" on the back of his shirt. Then Ned grumbled in his husky voice, "You been marked."

Ned rushed past Brent lying nearly unconscious on the floor and back down the hallway. He made his way back out the way he had come in. As he crawled out the window, he could hear the screams of the servants as they discovered the bloodbath he'd left behind.

CHAPTER ONE

Fifteen Years Later.

VICTORIA ROSE had recently become a regular customer at Dion O'Boyle's florist shop. With her glowing auburn hair and distinctly attractive features, O'Boyle never failed to remark that she was "the most beautiful flower in his shop." She had endured plays on her last name her entire life, but O'Boyle was a kindly man with a gentle demeanor and it was clear that he meant it as a compliment. And since he was also head of the North Side underworld gang, he could say just about anything he wanted. With his neatly parted brown hair, tweed jacket, pressed trousers, and ever-present pocket watch, you certainly wouldn't have known it by looking at him.

O'Boyle couldn't help but notice that she wasn't much like his other usual customers, who came every day in pretty dresses and expensive jewelry. Now that it was Spring and the flowers were in bloom, he greatly looked forward to their daily visits. Each was as lovely and poised as the one before, like his own personal procession of Ziegfeld Girls. Vicky, however, was more business-like: smartly dressed in a tan skirt and jacket, never any jewelry, and very light on the cosmetics. She'd told him that she was an office secretary, but he was sure she'd have a better chance of landing her boss for a husband with a change of wardrobe. What's more, she always arrived in the afternoon, when most secretaries usually came in early, during their morning errands.

O'Boyle watched her casually stroll around the shop, never in a hurry. Despite her attire, his gaze instinctively followed her every move. She hovered in her usual area and perused among the daisies, carnations, and gladiolus — always the most inexpensive flowers. Whoever her mysterious employer was, O'Boyle reasoned, he didn't mind her taking a long time to shop for flowers, but he was certainly cheap.

Eventually, she would glance at her watch, determine it was time to leave, then carelessly grab a small bouquet before dashing out.

This time it was daisies.

"Will this do it for you, Miss Rose?" he asked with a friendly smile.

"Yes, Mr. O'Boyle, thank you," she replied politely.

"Are you sure I couldn't interest you in some roses this time?" he queried. "Your boss might enjoy the change from all the daisies. Besides, they fit you so perfectly."

"Oh, no, but thank you just the same," she answered. "These will do just fine."

Such a puzzling girl, he thought, as he leaned on the counter and scratched his chin. If she'd been a man, he might have thought she was "casing the joint." Again, his eyes instinctively followed as she rushed out the door, climbed into the her tan, two-door coupe, and sped off to who-knows-where.

O'BOYLE would have been quite surprised to learn that *where* was actually the city room of the *Daily Crusader*, where Vicky, as one of the few woman reporters on staff, worked the City Hall beat. One that she was desperate to escape.

The hurried clack of her heels on the hardwood floor was virtually inaudible from the constant symphony of typewriters that echoed through the newsroom. Vicky quickly scanned the newsroom for a desk that *didn't* already have any flowers and eyeballed Perry Phillips two rows away. He was clumsy and bespectacled, and always wore a sweater vest no matter the weather. She could run rings around him any day of the week. But he had one advantage over her — he was a man (if not a very manly one).

She grabbed one of the dozen or more cheap, plastic vases she had handy and dumped the bouquet beside his typewriter.

"Merry Christmas," she said flatly.

He immediately stopped typing.

"Hey, Vick," he asked, "what's with all the flowers?"

"Just trying to brighten up the place, is all," she replied, and threw in a cutesy smile for good effect. She figured she could just blame it on "girlyness" and that would suffice. She figured right.

Phillips mumbled an unintelligible response and went back to his typing.

Vicky checked her watch and was just about to head for the door when City Editor Frank Matson bolted from his office and quickly scanned the room like a dog on the hunt. She'd been there long enough to know that look. Frank had a hot story and he needed someone to bring it home. Unfortunately, that look never landed on her. It was tough enough for woman reporters, but it was impossible for a gal to get on the crime beat. But that didn't keep her from trying. She bolted straight for his office, ready to take the ball.

Frank was a newsman, through and through. He sat behind that large mahogany desk every day, sleeves rolled up, tie pulled loose (he never bothered to tie it, even when he put it on) and the jacket that he never wore hung behind his desk. He was still tough for a middle-aged man, having earned his way up on the crime beat himself. No matter how long he spent behind a desk, he could smell a good story from a mile away, and yearned to savor every detail of a sordid narrative.

"Phillips!" Frank barked as he looked straight past her.

"Yes, Frank?" Phillips called, spilling his coffee and grabbing his notebook. Phillips rushed over to Frank's side and listened intently as he unsuccessfully fished his pockets for a pencil.

"Phillips," Frank dictated, "the Greenhill Warehouse down on Dock Street just found a barrel with a body stuffed inside."

Phillips turned green as he continued to search for any kind of writing utensil.

"Wow, we haven't had one of those in years," Vicky remarked as she inserted herself into the conversation.

"Get down there right away before the cops lock everybody out," Frank commanded to Phillips.

Vicky calmly reached into her inside jacket pocket and handed Phillips a pen as she made her move. "Come on, Frank, why don't you let me take this one? I promise I'll get the whole scoop. Wrap it up in a nice little bow, for you, too."

Phillips just stood there, not knowing what to do.

"What are you waiting for?" Frank shouted to Phillips with a pointed stare. "Get on it!" He had refused to even acknowledge that Vicky was there. He turned on his heel and whirled back into his office.

Phillips quickly turned for the door and ran smack into a desk on his way out.

She got the message, but that didn't mean she had to accept it. She was right on Frank's footsteps.

"Listen, Frank," she pleaded as she followed him into his office. As soon as Frank plopped down in his chair, she grabbed the arm rests and leaned over him. If nothing else, she thought the view might help her plea. She knew he was a devoted family man, but she was never above using her feminine wiles to get what she wanted. "You know I can run rings around Phillips. He'll probably go to the wrong warehouse. If you really want that story, then give it to me! You won't regret it."

"Forget it, Red," he answered, as he determinedly looked the other way. "I told you a million times, the crime beat is no place for a woman. Besides, the election is coming up, and you've already got an interview with Alderman Nibley this afternoon. Now get out of here."

"Come on, Frank," she continued. Everybody knows Nibley doesn't stand a snowball's chance, and he's squeaky clean to boot. I'm tired of cooling my heels with the old dogs in City Hall. I'm ready to move up!"

Frank just shook his head. "Look Red, even if you weren't a woman, you're still too green. You've got to cut your teeth somewhere. So get back down to City Hall and bring me that interview, Pronto. It's going in the morning edition."

"Aye aye, Captain," she said with a disappointed salute, then sulked her way out. She was just barely out the door when Frank shouted one more command.

"And one more thing! Stop bringing in all these flowers! It's starting to look like a greenhouse in here!"

RUNNING for re-election, again, was incumbent Mayor E. Leland Tackman. Tackman was well connected, and well financed, and it was in the best interest for many parties throughout the city that he serve yet another term. Well suspected, but certainly never proven, was the fact that one of those interested parties was Big Jack Torrisimo. He most likely topped the list of "silent contributors."

The challenger to this "well greased" system was local businessman and Alderman John Nibley. Nibley had done well for himself in the insurance business, and wanted to "give back to the community." Like many, he felt that the corruption in the Mayor's office was a good place to start. He'd served a few terms on the City Council, certainly enough to understand how the wheels turned, and now he was ready to really make a difference. Nibley had the wherewithal — and the finances — to attempt to do something about it. Perhaps the only thing he lacked was the good sense to tell himself that this was not an idea that could succeed.

Vicky sat down with Nibley in his office at City Hall for her first-ever interview with someone of near importance. With every question she asked, Nibley stayed on target with his canned response of how Tackman had been under the thumb of Big Jack Torrisimo and the Mob for years, how his office was full of corruption, and that he planned to do something about it.

"But, Mr. Nibley, aren't you a part of that office?" Vicky asked.

Nibley was not to be deterred. "I'm glad you asked that. I certainly have been a part of this office, and it has, thankfully, allowed me to see first-hand just what kind of corruption has been going on here. It's opened my eyes to exactly what needs to be done and how we can return honesty to government. Our government."

Vicky then tried another direction. "Mr. Nibley, there's a lot of people in this city who fear the influence of the Mob. A lot of people say that Tackman is on Big Jack's payroll. What do we do about that? Is there anything we *can* do?"

Nibley smiled and stayed on point. "That's a very good question and it clearly shows the influence that the Mob has had in this city's political system." Vicky didn't even bother to write down the rest of his answer.

Judging by his responses alone, Nibley sounded just as full of hot air as any other politician. But beyond the simple words, there was an honesty, a sincerity, and a true conviction behind his voice that made her think he might have actually believed the things he was saying. As a reporter, even a junior one, Vicky had long ago learned not to trust anyone at their word, but she liked Mr. John Nibley, and secretly felt in her heart that he should win. She thought that she might even vote for him. Unlike a good reporter though, she let that thought show in her next question.

"That's really quite noble," Mr. Nibley. "But how do you run an honest campaign when you're up against an opponent like Tackman?"

"Of course," concluded Nibley, moving off script and finally opening up and speaking completely from the heart, "I realize I don't stand much of a chance against Tackman. But I feel deep in my heart that someone has to try. That's one thing my father always told me. You can never get anywhere in life if you don't ever try."

It was a heart-felt plea, and one that certainly appealed to her. The election was only a few days away, and by then the whole city would decide whether or not to give someone like Nibley a chance to fight the good fight, or continue with the status quo. But as she thought earlier, it was already a forgone conclusion. That was too bad.

THE NIGHT before the election, Vicky settled in for a relaxing evening in her room at Mrs. Hershey's Boarding House for Women. It was a quaint and cozy place, rather Victorian — a bit too strict for her tastes, and too confining for someone with her independent streak, but it was safe and she knew that her place would be well looked after. Mrs. Hershey never missed a detail.

The previous week had been long and eventful, and Vicky was ready to relax. The election was a nice diversion from the usual grind, but she was ready to move on. It would soon be behind her, and with her endless visits to the flower shop (which she gambled would pay off soon, certainly before she went broke buying flowers), she hoped to make more inroads with Frank on moving over to the crime beat.

That was when the phone rang out in the hall. It was Frank, breathless and in a state of panic. "Vicky! Glad I caught you! Everyone else is out. I need you to get down to the Lexington right away!"

The Lexington, as Vicky well knew, was where Tackman had his campaign headquarters. Her reporter's instincts told her that something must have happened during the pre-election festivities for Frank to call in such a panic.

She barely got out the words to ask what it was before Frank quickly interrupted with the answer. "Tackman's dead! Heart attack! A little bird told me he died a happy man, if you know what I mean. They had to get him dressed and move him to another room before they could call the police. I need you to get over there, pronto!"

Vicky barely hung up the phone before she grabbed her jacket and raced out the door. Mrs. Hershey watched from the window as Vicky jumped in her small coupe and sped off into the night. Trouble must be brewing, she thought. She'd only have to wait until the morning's headlines to find out just how much.

Thanks to the lateness of the hour, Vicky made it over to The Lexington in record time. It was an immense, luxurious hotel in the better part of town. The Lexington was known for its grand ballrooms, crystal chandeliers, and expensive suites. Vicky had always wanted to see the inside, and to-night she would get her chance. Unfortunately, the place was surrounded by police, reporters, and more bystanders than she'd seen in her life. Getting in would be tricky. But she excelled at tricky.

She rushed around to the back and found more reporters at the rear entrance. She kept moving further around the building until she found exactly the door she was looking for — the service entrance. There was no one around, but it only opened from the inside. No ordinary reporter could ever get in here, either, but Vicky was no ordinary reporter. She stuck her Press Pass in her purse, loosened her blouse, fluffed her hair, and knocked softly.

Right away, she heard a disgruntled voice on the other side. "I already told you people to back off," shouted a large, surly Busboy as he flung open the door, spoiling for a fight, or at least scaring some unsuspecting reporter into thinking he was. He stopped short when he spotted Vicky looking up at him with pouty lips, sultry eyes, and those amazingly arched eyebrows. "Not another one."

"They told me to come back here," she cooed. Vicky knew full well that even when a hotel is wrapped up tight in a crisis, certain things just never stopped. And they always used the service entrance.

The Busboy looked around, grabbed her by the hand and pulled her quickly inside. The door slammed shut behind them.

"So strong," Vicky purred as she brushed up against him. "Thank you."

He did his best to keep his composure. It wasn't easy. "So, you know where to go?"

"Oh, yeah. But maybe you can show me some other time." She left him with that thought as she sauntered down the plain, tiled hallway. That was too easy.

She found the service elevator in no time and headed straight for the floor (which had been widely reported in the papers) where the Tackman headquarters was encamped. Seemed as good a place as any to start. Tackman had been getting on in years, overweight, and privileged. He liked people coming to him. She figured that he wouldn't stray too far from his campaign suite for a "private meeting with one of his beloved constituents."

As luck would have it once again, the hallway was quiet and clear of people when the service elevator reached Tackman's floor. Finally getting her first real look at the hotel, she wasn't disappointed. The plush carpet felt like a cushion beneath her shoes. She really wanted to take them off and feel it with her bare feet. The wallpaper was more ornate that anything she'd ever seen. Even the hallway felt like a palace.

Vicky knew she didn't have time to revel in her surroundings. She quickly got her bearings and headed down the hall, looking for Tackman's suite.

There were three other rooms in the immediate vicinity. She stopped at the first one and listened, but heard nothing. Before she could get her ear to the next, she heard someone coming out. There was no time to hide, or even step away before the door swung open and she found herself staring face to face with Vito Spats. Luck, it seemed, had just left her high and dry.

Vito Spats looked at her coldly, then said, "She's right in here. Hurry up, get in here." With an even firmer grip than the Busboy, Vito Spats grabbed her by the arm and tugged her inside, closing the door at the same time with one fluid motion. This was getting to be familiar. It only took her a second to think of how to respond.

"So strong. Thank you." After all, it had worked the first time.

Vito Spats looked back at her, gave her the once-over, but didn't exactly warm up. "I'll be back in a few minutes." He opened the door just an inch, then checking to make sure the hallway was clear, left as quickly as he'd pulled her in.

Vicky rushed into the room and found a beautiful young girl, possibly over eighteen (more likely not), sitting on the bed, crying in quiet hysterics. She was only half dressed, her mascara running down her face. Vicky knelt down beside her. The silk sheets sure felt good. Any other time she would have loved to throw herself across the bed and wrap herself up in them from head to toe.

The girl stopped sobbing long enough to ask, "Who are you?"

"I've come to get you out of here," Vicky replied, pulling herself together. But not before she stole a quick look at the enormous bathroom with a tub that she could swim in for hours. The girl nodded, aware of the agreement Vicky had apparently stumbled into.

"What's your name?" Vicky asked.

"Susan," the girl managed to get out.

"Can you get dressed?" Vicky continued. Susan nodded again and obediently reached for her blouse on the bed.

Vicky grabbed the phone and prayed that Frank would be waiting and ready to act on the other end. He was. She told him to meet them a block away from the rear side of the hotel and to get there as fast as he could. Frank knew better than to ask any questions. He hung up before she did. Vicky needed just one more piece of luck this night, and fortunately, the paper was only a few blocks away. It was going to hit the fan soon, and she wanted to make doubly sure that she and Susan weren't there when it did.

CHAPTER TWO

AFTER throwing her jacket around Susan's shoulders, it only took a few minutes before Vicky had them down the service elevator and headed back towards the service entrance. Susan followed dutifully behind. Either she'd been through this before and knew just what she was expected to do, or had never been through anything like this before and was more than willing to put her trust in Vicky to get her through it. Vicky was more than certain it was the latter.

She hoped that they wouldn't run into her Busboy on the way out, but there he was, keeping his vigilant post at the outside door. She reasoned that he must have been given orders to keep watch and not to let anyone in. Any reporters, anyway. Vicky was all set to go into her act again when, without a word, the Busboy dutifully opened the door and guided them right out. Vicky shot him an over-appreciative smile as the door quickly shut behind them.

Keeping up her momentum, she tugged Susan through the bushes to the narrow alley behind the hotel. They kept a quick and steady pace until they reached the street on the opposite block. Just like clockwork, Frank pulled up in his car. Vicky gave a quick look around as she opened the door and gently pushed Susan inside. It was all clear. No one had seen. Her final bit of luck had held out.

Frank never said a word, though she knew he was probably bursting inside and full of questions as he drove them across town to the Sherman, a hotel that was on the paper's payroll. Naturally, this one paled in comparison to The Lexington. They took the back entrance to a modestly-furnished suite on the top floor. Frank dutifully stayed outside as Vicky led Susan into the room, fixed her a drink, and got her as comfortable as possible. Susan needed a friendly ear, and Vicky was all prepared to lend her one.

As much as Frank wanted to come in and hear all the juicy details first-hand, he knew Vicky would have a much better chance alone. Knowing they were safe and secure, he headed out to an all-night diner to grab a bite and kill time before checking back in a few hours.

"Oh, it was horrible! Just horrible! There we were, having a good time, when he just sat upright, moaning like he'd been shot in the back or something. Then he just fell over! Then this stuff came out of his mouth — it wasn't blood. I don't know what it was. I just kept screaming and I ran out in the hall. It was just so horrible!"

Vicky sat down next to her, held her tight and dried her tears. She told Susan that everything was going to be okay, that she would take care of her. Susan cried her heart out and over the next several hours spilled every sordid detail of the event, all the events that had come before that one, and just how she'd come to be in such a place to begin with.

Susan told how she'd left home a few years earlier and moved to Terminal City to live with an aunt. Being a naturally pretty girl, she'd found some work as a catalogue model and then achieved her one claim to fame doing advertisements for a tire company. "I was Miss Lotta Miles." But times were tough and even modeling work was hard to come by. That was when she met "an exceedingly nice fellow," Albert Ronga (Vicky knew the name) who told her that she could do quite well as an escort. "He said I could easily earn enough money to go to New York or Hollywood in no time. Sadly, I was too naive at the time to know what he actually meant, or that he worked for Big Jack Torrisimo."

Despite what she did, even out of desperation, Susan felt she could have ended up a lot worse. Due to her looks and her fame as a model, she only "dated" the most influential men in town. Actually, she felt a sense of pride in being the Mayor's favorite girl. "And Mr. Kennelly's, too," she beamed. And she'd nearly saved up enough money for that trip to Hollywood.

Vicky shook her head inside, but smiled agreeably, thinking to herself, "Wow, the favorite of the rich and the powerful. That should really impress those casting agents."

It was many hours later before Vicky finally stepped out into the hall and, just as she suspected, found Frank sitting there, back from the diner and waiting. "John Brown it! It's about time."

Vicky repeated everything she'd learned, not sparing a single detail and making a few of the less exciting ones sound even better, as they went to the office. Frank told her she'd done great, that she could go home now and he'd write up the story, but give her full credit. Vicky insisted on typing it herself. She quickly banged it out on the spare typewriter they kept in a nearby room, though not without error.

As they pulled up at The Lexington a few hours and several cups of coffee later to retrieve her car, Vicky stared up at the hotel in awe. "Frank," she confessed, "I know you're one-hundred percent devoted to Betty and the girls, but if you ever wanted to have me, one night at The Lexington is all it'd take."

Frank stared back at her curiously as she hopped out of the car. "Now that the heat's died down, I can go grab a peak at the lobby," she said as she dashed off. Frank shook his head as he drove off. It had been a very long night. Despite Vicky's offer, he couldn't wait to get back home to Betty.

Vicky swung by the Carousel on her way home, but they were long closed. She peered through the windows to see if perhaps Jerry was still cleaning up, but no such luck. She sure could have used a double chocolate before going home.

She woke up late the next morning to the sound of the Newsboys still hawking the morning edition. "TACKMAN DIES; NIBLEY WINS!" She heard later that hundreds of people had actually made it to the voting booths before they read the news. And of course, the *Daily Crusader* had the whole scoop about just what had happened in that hotel room the night before, straight from the horse's mouth.

Vicky couldn't help but feel a sense of pride; that justice had prevailed. Nibley had won the election by default.

Sometimes, it pays to try.

MAYOR-ELECT Nibley granted his first interview to one reporter and one reporter only: Victoria Rose of the *Daily Crusader*. In the interview, Nibley repeated his promise to root the corruption out of City Hall.

"I'm going to clean up Terminal City and run Big Jack out of town if it takes everything I've got!" Of course, now that the election was over, everyone felt that Nibley would forget this foolish crusade and would eventually fall under the thumb of Big Jack Torrisimo, just as his predecessors had. Only time would tell, and in all likelihood, it would do so quickly.

Interested parties, however, weren't interested in waiting to find out. As Nibley worked late in his office one night, he found a man standing in his doorway. With his bowler hat and gleaming white spats, he was too well-dressed to be a hoodlum. But he wasn't dressed quite well enough to not be. His friends and his enemies all knew him as "Vito Spats." Nibley, too, knew exactly who he was.

Vito had a message for him. He didn't say from whom it came. He didn't have to. "You made a lot of big promises getting here. Election's over now, so you'll cooperate if you knows what's good for you. Things run a certain way in Terminal City, and its time you learned the ropes."

Nibley looked back at Vito Spats defiantly. "I'm here to cut those very ropes."

Vito smirked on his way out, "Well then, we'll see who gets cut."

WITH the election over, Vicky resumed her daily visits to Dion O'Boyle's florist shop. With the office filling up and Frank's admonition, she'd taken to just handing them out on the street. She'd also gotten more than one poor fellow in trouble when a suspicious wife wondered why a pretty girl had just handed her husband flowers out of the blue.

As Vicky browsed through the lilies, honeysuckle, and

periwinkle in the back of the store, she heard the bell on the shop door announce the arrival of a new customer. She glanced through the petals to see two large men enter, one of which wore a bowler hat, waxed moustache, and gleaming white spats. Despite his posh attire, Vicky knew exactly who he was — Vito Spats. No doubt about it. The other, in a tweed vest with shiny brass buttons, she didn't know. One look at the reddish tip of his bulbous nose told her she'd certainly remember him.

O'Boyle greeted the men warmly, as he always did his customers, extending a hand to shake. Vito Spats took O'Boyle's hand in a vice-like grip as the other Soldato quickly jammed a small revolver firmly into his abdomen and shot him three times. The sound was partially muffled by the folds of O'Boyle's tweed vest and jacket.

Vicky jolted back in horror, knocking into the plants behind her. Vito Spats looked in her direction before the two men walked out of the store just as quickly as they had entered. She watched through the window as they stepped into a waiting car and drove away.

Vicky rushed to O'Boyle's side and had to step around the growing pool of blood that flowed beneath him. From the cold, grimaced look on his face, it was clear that he was already dead. There was nothing she could do to help.

She bolted from the store and looked up and down the sidewalk. People just strolled by, completely unaware of the execution that had just taken place. On the street corner, the local Beat Cop was talking to two young boys. Life was going on, with no one the wiser.

Vicky rushed to her car and got her camera bag. She would call out to the Beat Cop in a few minutes, but first she was going to get some photographs of the crime scene. This was just the opportunity she needed. Word on the street had been that O'Boyle was going to get hit. And now she was the only witness. Her persistence had finally paid off.

Vicky rushed back into the shop, locked the door, and turned the sign to "Closed." She couldn't believe her amazing luck (or O'Boyle's bad luck) as she snapped photos of the crime scene, throwing her spent bulbs into a nearby trash can. She wasn't the best photographer, she knew, but given her subject, she really couldn't take a bad angle.

The Closed sign didn't get anyone's attention, but the flash from her camera certainly did. She had just completed her last shot when she heard an elderly woman scream outside the store. She turned around to see a dozen noses pressed against the glass, eyes glued to the gruesome scene before them like a display in a department store window. The old woman's scream was quickly followed by the sound of the Beat Cop's whistle.

Vicky unlocked the door and easily slipped out in the hubbub as a throng of people pushed their way in, with the Beat Cop closely behind. She dashed back to her car and, tossing the camera bag in the passenger seat, drove off in the same manner as the assassins had done just a few minutes before. She'd gotten *her* shots, too. Now it was time for her glory.

Her first impulse was to run down to the closest soda shop and celebrate with a double chocolate malt, her drink of choice and her one true vice. Given a choice between living and living without her double chocolates — well, that would have been a hard choice indeed. But on this day, there was one thing that actually outweighed a double chocolate — the chance to gloat. She would have even more to celebrate later.

CHAPTER THREE

FRANK gave a whistle as he looked through the photographs.

"How in John Brown's name did you get these, Red?" Frank had promised his wife that he'd give up swearing and cited the name of John Brown whenever he felt the urge.

Vicky smiled, still reeling from her own ingenuity. "Vito Spats has been feeling his oats lately, and I figured no matter what Big Jack said, he was going to make a move on O'Boyle. O'Boyle's always on his guard except when he's working in his shop. Vito Spats never gets out before ten o'clock, and with traffic it's a good half-hour drive or more for him to get there. I figured he'd make a move sometime after lunch while the shop was slow, before things picked up near quitting time. Pretty simple, really. Lucky for me, no one pays any attention to a gal hanging around a flower shop."

"Where'd you learn all that?" Frank asked, his gaze still fixed on the photos.

"The paper. You should try reading it sometime," Vicky smirked.

Frank stopped looking at the photos long enough to fume for a moment. "Red, how many times do I have to tell you? You're supposed to be down at City Hall —"

Vicky jumped in before he could finish. "City Hall? Look at these pictures!"

Frank jumped right back in where he left off. "— Not spending time in a flower shop waiting around for somebody to get shot. I keep telling you, the crime beat is no place for a gal."

"Come on, Frank!" Vicky shot back. "This *woman* just scooped every paper in town. Including this one! I was there. The only witness! And I had the whole place to myself when I got these shots."

Frank sat back in his chair, dumbfounded. She was right. He'd have killed to get an opportunity like this one. "So how did it go down? Did you see it?"

"Sure did. Vito Spats shook O'Boyle's hand and got him in the death grip while the other one pumped him full of lead. Three shots to the gut."

Frank almost swooned at the details. "I'll be John Brown." Then his brow furrowed a bit, worried for her. "Did they see you?"

"I was in the back of the store. They knew I was there, but they didn't come after me. I don't think they even got a good look at me. I was behind some plants. I'm sure they thought I was just a customer."

Frank sat back in his chair again. This was too much for him. "Okay, Red. I want you to go over the whole story again. And don't leave out any details. How much blood was there? Did he have a grimaced look on his face? Did he die right away?"

AFTER recounting the gory details, some gorier than they had been in real-life, Vicky kept her unofficial appointment at the Carousel — the soda fountain on her way home and her usual hangout after hours. "Burn one all the way," was the shout for a double chocolate malt. It was music to her ears. The gleaming white walls and red-topped tables were her idea of heaven.

At the Carousel, the folks there usually knew when to expect her and Jerry, the owner, would set one in front of her as soon as she parked herself on the stool. Jerry could always tell right away whether she was drinking to celebrate or trying to forget. To-night she was clearly celebrating.

The never-ending grin as she unwrapped the paper from her straw was a dead give-away. "Thank you, Jerry. You're a Saint."

"We do our best," Jerry shrugged. He was a solid, reliable-looking fellow. Even with his white paper hat and apron, though, he wasn't the kind you'd expect to be running a soda shop. With his crew cut, muscular arms, and tattoos that sometimes snuck out from under his rolled-up sleeves, he looked more like a Marine Drill Sergeant. Vicky always wondered what a guy like him was doing dishing ice cream from behind a counter, but she'd never been forward enough to ask. This night, though, she didn't even think about it.

"So, good news to-day?" Jerry asked, knowing the answer.

"Oh, yeah," she smiled as she drove the straw into the tall glass and took her first long sip. It was chocolate heaven.

"So, what's the scoop?" Jerry asked.

Vicky gave him a mischievous grin as she took another long sip. "You'll just have to wait 'till you see the front page to-morrow."

THE NEXT morning, Vicky returned to City Hall with renewed vigor. The boys at the Mayor's office would think of her differently now that she had a byline on the biggest crime story to come down the pike in a while. Especially Bill Higgs, the old codger of a reporter who worked for the *Terminal City Standard*. But then again, Higgs would probably dislike her even more.

Vicky had looked at the morning edition long enough to peruse her pictures and see her name under the headline. "O'BOYLE DEAD IN GANGLAND SHOOTING," by Victoria Rose. First time a gal had ever had a byline on the front page of the *Crusader*, or any other paper in Terminal City for that matter. Boy, did that ever sing! She'd scanned the first few paragraphs before having to stop and finish getting ready before dashing out the door. She didn't want to be late for her chance to rub it in.

"So Boys, seen the morning paper to-day?" she asked as she strolled into the tiny, cramped room on the basement floor at City Hall. Though the four-story brick building was finely furnished from the first floor up, their sparse office had only a few desks and telephones. Not even a girly calendar. The one narrow window was situated near the ceiling and provided a tiny glimpse of the grassy lawn outside. She made sure to clack her high heels extra loud to make certain they knew she was coming. The men were quick to their feet, offering her praise and wishing her the best.

Except for Bill Higgs, of course. "So, how'd you manage to be in that flower shop at just the right time, eh?" He asked through sneering eyes.

"Spent a lot of time looking at flowers, and buying more than I could ever need. Should have brought you a bouquet, Higgs," she told him.

"All sounds pretty suspicious to me," Higgs replied, breathing sharply through his nose. "Pretty suspicious." He sat back down at his desk, his too-large rumpled suit nearly swallowing him.

Morty Cohen, a fatherly gent from the *Standard*, and the one who was always first to come to Vicky's side, chimed in. "Come on, Bill, this is the girl's big moment. You can at least offer her a kind thought. Admit when somebody else does good. Besides, when have you ever been scooped by somebody so pretty before?"

Higgs just grumbled again, "Pretty suspicious."

"So, Vicky, the Cops got any idea who did it?" Morty asked, sitting back down, careful not to crease his brown slacks. Morty was as neat as he was kind.

Vicky looked back in surprise. "Oh, yeah. It was Vito Spats. Didn't you read the article?"

The men returned the look of surprise. "Vito Spats? Are you sure about that?"

Morty flipped through the paper again. "There's nothing in here about him."

Vicky grabbed the paper again and breezed through the article. Morty was right. The look on her face told the others exactly what they suspected. The best part of her story, the part that fingered one of the killers, had been edited out.

Vicky wheeled around and was at the door in an instant,

without even saying good-bye. Her heels clacked the floor even louder on her way out. But this time, the loudness wasn't for them.

It was for Frank.

FRANK knew she was coming before she ever stormed into his office and waved the morning edition in his face. Not even the sound of every typewriter in the office could have drowned out the din from her heels as she stormed down the hall.

Only he had no idea what could have made her so upset. He thought she'd still be celebrating.

"Frank! What in the Dickens do mean by cutting my story? How could you do that to me?" she shouted before she grabbed the name plate off of his desk and hurled it towards his head. Luckily, he managed to duck just in time.

"John Brown it!" Frank shouted as he recaptured his wits.

Frank had to think a moment to put it together. "What, you mean the part about Vito Spats?"

The burst of fire in her eyes told him that he'd hit the mark. "How could you do that? This was my scoop!"

Frank stood up, trying his best to calm her down, and grabbed his paper weight before she could get her hands on it. "Red, we report the news here, that's all. We don't take on the Mob! Now, they already know there was a witness. You want them to know it was you?"

"I'm not afraid, Frank," she shot back defiantly.

"Well, then, you're just plain crazy," he replied. "You remember Richard Potter? How he went on a crusade against Big Jack a few years ago? Ran a different article just about every day? Remember? They shot him down in cold blood, right out in front of the building. You should think twice about that before you go shooting your mouth off about what you saw. You may think this is just a story, a way to boost yourself up the ladder, but these people don't operate under the same rules. This is why I keep telling you, Red, the crime beat is no place for a woman. I did it for your own good."

She stopped long enough for his words to sink in, and

realized that they did, in fact, make sense.

"I suppose you're right."

"Now, have you told anyone else yet?" Frank asked, worried.

"Just the boys down at City Hall."

"Well, then play it smart, Red. Don't let it get any further, okay?" Frank told her, worriedly. "And don't even think about going to the police. Big Jack has practically the entire force on the payroll. You squawk down there and it'll get back to Big Jack faster than you can call Western Union."

She looked up at him and saw, for the first time, the concern in his face. Yes, Frank was a newsman, through and through. He'd do just about anything for a story. But he wouldn't sacrifice one of his reporters to get it.

Especially her.

CHAPTER FOUR

DION O'BOYLE'S funeral brought the city to a standstill. Mob funerals in Terminal City were a macabre contest in which each fallen boss' importance was measured by the size of his procession. The more important the boss, the bigger the procession. Therefore, each boss (or rather, the boss' underlings), attempted to outdo the previous Mob funeral by a recognizable amount.

O'Boyle's funeral was no exception. His was measured against that of Michael Memoli, the leader of the Terminal City Italian League who, oddly enough, had died of cancer the previous month. Memoli's funeral was easily "the biggest the city had ever seen" at the time, but O'Boyle's was clearly bigger.

The casket cost over $10,000. It was made of silver and bronze and surrounded on all sides with gold candlesticks (the funeral parlor even assigned a young man to accompany the casket at all times to keep the candles lit and quickly replace any before they burned out). On the top was a gold tablet that read "Dion O'Boyle, 1904-1936."

The funeral procession to the Mount Carmel cemetery was easily a mile long, with more than two-dozen overflowing cars and trucks just to carry the flowers. Every big-time florist and small-time flower shop in the city had worked overtime to create the largest funeral wreaths the city had ever seen. Like with the funeral itself, every mobster in town was determined to outdo both his enemies and compatriots in crime. By the day of the burial, there wasn't a single flower or bud of any kind to be found in the entire city. Some shops even had to have flowers shipped in to meet the orders.

Among the many wreaths, standing sprays, hearts, and crosses, two particular arrangements stood out. One was a life-size effigy of O'Boyle himself, with an eerie-looking wax head and a blue suit made completely of flowers. The other was a large basket of twelve dozen red and white roses with a card that read simply, "FROM JACK."

The procession and burial included 15,000 mourners and was so large it quickly gained national attention. Not to mention fascination. It extended for more than a mile and included three marching bands and a last-minute police escort from the nearby town of Lennox. The day before the parade, Terminal City Chief of Police Harry LaSalle realized it would be rather embarrassing for a large contingent of his own force to participate.

Vicky, Frank, and the rest of the employees at the *Daily Crusader* lined up at the second floor open windows to watch the procession go by. The streets were filled with onlookers and Vicky was amazed that there were that many people left to *watch* the funeral considering just how many people were actually *in* it.

Vicky asserted that the send-off was clearly bigger than that of Michael Memoli. Perry Phillips added that Memoli was the only Mob leader who'd died of natural causes that he could ever remember. Frank chuckled in agreement.

The best part of the procession for Vicky was the chance to get a first-hand look at all the major crime players in the city. What better opportunity, she thought, than to have them gathered in one group and march right past the offices of the *Crusader*, as her newshound companions provided a running commentary of just who was who. For someone so desperate to get onto the crime beat, this was an unbelievable occasion.

At the head of the parade were the six pallbearers, led by O'Boyle's successor and the new boss of the North Side gang, Jimmy "Nails" McCarthy. McCarthy was a broad-shouldered, dapper Irishman with a slight paunch and a tuft of thick hair who could have easily passed for any run-of-the-mill businessman. McCarthy's reputation, however, certainly outweighed his appearance and there were many in the city who feared that his ascension would bring about more gang violence. It was a justified fear.

McCarthy earned his nickname as a young street hood for his "tough-as-nails" attitude and fighting skill. He was so quick with his fists that he could usually handle three-to-four opponents on his own. After beating several members of a Polish gang to death with a baseball bat, he was given a choice: go to prison or join the Army and fight in the Great War. McCarthy chose the Army and was sent to France, where his superiors promoted him to sergeant after noting his natural leadership abilities and "unusual aptitude for weapons." The French government awarded him the *Croix de Guerre* for capturing twenty Germans and their machine gun in a dangerous trench raid. Jobs were scarce after the war, until McCarthy fell in with O'Boyle and helped to build his empire on the North Side.

Next to McCarthy was his new second-in-command, Eddie "Whitey" O'Leary. O'Leary was a soft-spoken man with pale skin (hence the moniker), strawberry blond hair, a quick sense of humor, and an itchy trigger finger. The newspapers portrayed him as a jolly good murderer who was always good for a chuckle and a quote. Usually both at the same time. One day he ran into a prominent judge and his wife at a baseball game and quipped, "Judge, that's a beautiful diamond ring your wife's wearing. If it's snatched some night, promise me you won't go hunting for me. I'm telling you now, I'm innocent!" But his enemies knew him as someone who would smile at you one minute, put a bullet in your head the next, and afterwards make a joke about it.

Close to Whitey was Nails' younger brother, Michael "Monk" McCarthy. He was known for sharing his older brother's killer instinct, but without the business panache. The younger McCarthy was taller and bulkier than his sibling. Numerous street fights as a kid had given him a broken nose and scarred jowls. His simian appearance and overall size gained him the nickname "Monk" from rival gangsters. He earned his stripes working as a bouncer in O'Boyle's various speakeasies during Prohibition. He usually strutted about with a large club, a sidearm in his coat, and brass knuckles on both fists. He enjoyed beating up unruly customers and for each knockout (or death) with his club, he would add a new notch. In less than a year he'd accumulated forty-nine notches. After counting them up one night, he clubbed an innocent man at the bar just to make it an even fifty.

Following them was a seemingly endless parade of North Side underlings, hangers on, and hired guns. Virtually everyone who'd had any kind of dealings for better or worse with O'Boyle was present.

Once the North Siders had all filed past the *Crusader* offices, Vicky leaned forward to get a better look at Big Jack Torrisimo and his South Side mob who controlled the area in which she lived and worked. If she ever made it to the crime beat, Vicky knew that she would have more run-ins with the South Side mobsters than any other hoodlums to be found in the city.

Vicky needed very little commentary for this group. She immediately recognized the lumbering, white-clad Big Jack at the front and especially his polished right-hand man, Vito Spats, who was largely responsible for the day's festivities. How he could walk in the funeral to honor the man he'd just killed was something that she just didn't understand. But, she figured, there would be a lot about the Mob that she wouldn't understand. With any luck, she would learn it all in time.

Next to Spats was someone else she recognized. The tweed vest and brass buttons were certainly enough of a give-away, but the bulbous, red-tinged nose confirmed his identity.

"There, that fellow with the red nose — he's the one who pulled the trigger on O'Boyle," she quickly alerted Frank. Frank peered over for a better look, but it wasn't really necessary to confirm the man's identity. The nose said it all.

"That's Milton Caifano, Vito Spats' right-hand man. They call him 'Cherry Nose,'" Frank explained.

"Sure you don't have to guess why," Phillips added with a chuckle.

Just then, as if he had heard them, Vito Spats looked up at their window. Vicky felt a chill run down her spine. It seemed like he was staring straight at her, though he couldn't possibly have been. She'd been well-hidden behind those plants and she was certain he couldn't have possibly singled her out, mixed in the group that lined the office windows.

But it definitely felt like he had looked up at her and none of her rationalizations made her feel any better about it. Vito Spats was not someone to be considered lightly.

That was something, she reminded herself, that she should never forget.

AS expected, the silence of the guns didn't last long.

On a quiet morning just days after the funeral, Big Jack walked confidently from his narrow, three-story brick home towards his waiting car where his young driver, Paulie Milano, stopped bouncing on his heels long enough to open the rear door. Paulie had only been Big Jack's driver for the past three months, having taken over from Jack's previous, long-time (and red-nosed) driver who'd recently been forced to escape the "heat" of Terminal City for the friendlier heat of Miami.

"How you doing, Paulie?" Big Jack asked in his usual low and matter-of-fact manner.

"Doing just great, Mr. Torrisimo," Paulie responded with as much joy and enthusiasm as he could muster. As much as it may have sounded so, it certainly wasn't an act. Paulie was as proud as he could be to have been named Big Jack's driver and saw nothing but rosy days ahead for his life within the organization. Things would only get better, of that he was sure.

Paulie dutifully shut the door behind Big Jack as the large man climbed inside and made himself comfortable. He then made another sweeping glance all around the neighborhood to make sure that all was clear. With the recent killing of Dion O'Boyle, he was well aware that a retaliatory attempt could be made on Big Jack, and the last thing he wanted was for it to happen on his watch. He wanted his future to stay rosy indeed.

Seeing that all was clear, Paulie jumped into the driver's seat and began the twelve-block route to Big Jack's restaurant, where the boss had an early appointment. He let out a small, inaudible sigh of relief, glad that he had Big Jack safe in the back seat. Because they took the precaution to vary their route from day to day, Paulie was sure that there was nothing much left to worry about until they arrived at their destination.

Or so he thought.

After they had gone several blocks, Paulie's comfort got the better of him. He failed to notice the black-curtained touring car that had cruised well behind them for some distance.

When they turned onto State Street, however, the car quickly gained speed and pulled right up alongside them. Big Jack only had a second to register the sight of the curtains being suddenly pulled open and catch the grimacing features of his would-be executioners as they stuck their Tommy guns out of the windows and rained a shower of bullets upon them like a storm of screaming hailstones. It was just enough time for Big Jack to dive to the floorboards as the shots ripped through his vehicle on every side and broken glass rained down around him like shattered crystal.

Paulie hit the gas as soon as the guns blazed their staccato rhythm, but it wasn't enough to save him. He never even had time to scream. He was already a shredded, bloody mess when their speeding car slammed into a light pole just a dozen yards away. The sudden stop tossed Big Jack forward against the long front seat. He stayed down in the floorboards and listened as the neighboring car sped off and disappeared.

Soon, it was quiet again.

Big Jack waited a few more very long minutes, just in case his attackers returned. When he was sure it was safe, he cautiously pried open the creaking, bullet-ridden door and slowly pulled his hulking figure from the twisted wreckage. Dots of blood stained the collar of his white shirt and jacket. A spray of Paulie's blood stained his right sleeve.

Big Jack peered around, careful to stay behind the car. There was no sign of his attackers. Surely, they must have thought him dead, or else they wouldn't have left so quickly.

Big Jack stepped back to get a better view of the car and said a quick Ave Maria. It looked just like the one that Bonnie and Clyde had ridden to their end just a few years earlier. Only their fates had been much different.

From his, at least.

It was a miracle that he was even alive. Much less with barely a scratch, except for a few cuts from broken glass.

He said another Ave Maria for Paulie. The kid never knew what hit him, he was sure of that. And he was also sure that he'd never again use an inexperienced driver.

Big Jack stared off in the direction in which he'd heard the car speed away and set his jaw. He knew who his attackers were. They made certain of that. They had wanted their faces to be the last ones he saw. That's why Whitey O'Leary and Monk McCarthy and had done the job themselves.

But there was one thing on which they hadn't counted.

Failure.

The Mob war had truly begun.

IN HIS first several weeks in office, Mayor Nibley held to his promise and began full steam on his clean-up operation. He had the Police organize raid after raid of the gambling dens, whorehouses, and illegal drinking parlors, shutting down many of Big Jack's operations and that of the North Side as well.

Nibley also went to work rooting out the corruption in the Police force, which was no small affair. Big Jack's pockets were rather deep, and his reach extended even deeper. For every Cop on the take that was ejected from the force, there were three more waiting, ready to be corrupted.

The Mob war was the only thing that continued unabated. Every week there seemed to be another execution as North and South Side minions were gunned down with increasing regularity. The only things that seemed to change were the armaments and location.

Nibley made for great copy, and even greater conversation.

Many people commented that Big Jack hadn't seen this much heat since the time "that handsome young D.A.," Thomas Gregor, went after him. These conversations most often ended with the words, "God rest his soul."

Many heralded Nibley as a savior, but some complained that he spent too much time on the Mob and not enough time worrying about the poverty that had stricken the city's people. The country was still in a depression, after all. Jobs were hard to come by and many families couldn't make ends meet. More and more people were going to the soup kitchens, looking for a hand out, anything that would carry them through another day. Big Jack may have been a bootlegger, panderer, and murderer, but he ran most of the soup kitchens in town and that good will went a long way with the city's poor. Big Jack clearly knew how to sway the court of public opinion. Like all mobsters before and after him, Big Jack knew well that with the law against him, he needed the huddled masses on his side. For that reason, he made doubly sure that the good people (well, most of them) of Terminal City thought of him as a Saint. With each arrest and editorial maligning his name, there came the accompanying, and much louder, public outcry.

"Big Jack is a good man!" they shouted. So he dabbled in a few vices? He was only giving the people what they wanted. "Look at all the good he was doing! If it weren't for Big Jack, many people would have starved!"

THE NEXT volley in the war between Big Jack and the Nails McCarthy's North Siders took place at Isadore Weiss' barber shop located on a corner just a few blocks from the hotel where Nails McCarthy made his home away from home.

McCarthy strongman and executioner Dennis Coonan strolled in late one afternoon for a shave. He had a much-anticipated date that evening with a certain lovely blond-haired temptress (who was not his wife, of course) and Coonan wanted to look his best.

"Ah, Mr. Coonan, welcome back!" Weiss greeted him with a smile and said in his heavy Lithuanian accent, "Please, sit down. My best chair, just for you."

Weiss turned the waiting chair towards Coonan and gave it a quick brush with a dry towel. "You have big plans tonight, eh? Something special, my friend?"

"As a matter of fact, I do," Coonan beamed. He'd been looking forward to this night for several days. He sat down in the chair and Weiss turned it back around towards the large mirror that covered the rear wall of the shop. As the Irish mobster leaned back with closed eyes to get comfortable, Weiss covered Coonan's face with a hot towel. In a near-stroke of odd fortune, the towel was too hot and Coonan let out a shout of surprise. He quickly pulled it from his face and Weiss grabbed it as he bowed apologetically.

"Mr. Coonan, please," Weiss pleaded as he grabbed the towel and backed away. "I am so sorry. Let me get you another."

"Just be careful next time," Coonan told him with a threatening tone. He sat back down just in time to see in the large mirror two men of olive complexion rush into the store with pistols at the ready.

Weiss gave a terrified shriek, shielded himself with one arm and ducked down in the very spot where he stood, as if that would have actually done him any good. Coonan had just enough time to jump from the chair and duck behind it before his assailant's pistols rang out in an explosive cacophony that quickly shattered the mirror and several bottles of hair tonic.

Coonan swung the chair back and forth to shield himself from his two attackers. It almost did the job. The first several rounds struck the chair or missed him completely. But the last few found their mark as the two men leaped around the twirling recliner and fired down on him from both sides.

Moments later, Coonan was a bullet-ridden heap on the tile floor. As his blood oozed out from beneath his body, it collected in the small piles of hair that were scattered about the floor.

His executioners wasted no time. They immediately rushed out of the store, jumped into a waiting car, and sped off.

Weiss stayed rooted to where he still kneeled down for

the longest time before his aging legs got the best of him and he was forced to stand up. It was only then that he realized that he was unharmed. Physically, at least.

He whimpered silently as he looked around at the mess that surrounded him. His store was in shattered pieces and the only thing worse was the massacred corpse that lay on the floor before him. He had to take two steps back to keep the blood from staining his only pair of leather shoes.

It would be a long time before he would reopen. But at least until then he would be free of their weekly graft payments that practically bled him dry.

Or so he hoped.

BIG JACK'S contributions to the poor and whether or not he was just "giving the people what they wanted" was a topic that Vicky and the boys in the press room discussed frequently. Vicky was always staunchly against corruption, no matter how friendly a face it wore, and even if the citizenry were willing accomplices. Surprisingly, Higgs actually agreed with her, and was fond of repeatedly quoting William Vanderbilt on the matter: "The public be damned!" (though he was completely mistaken on the context).

After one particularly long day, they carried their conversation to a nearby bar (though Vicky would have preferred a soda shop) where they kicked back for the evening. Morty, being his usual generous self, picked up the tab.

Being reporters in City Hall, they knew well the extent of complaint mail that Nibley was getting. Higgs pointed out that a fair number came from one Harvey O'Donnell, a family man and father of two. "Sent two more threatening letters this week. That last one sure sounds like he's got it out for the Mayor. I don't know why the police don't go pick that fellow up."

Vicky begged to differ. "You don't know it was a threat."

Higgs countered, "Well, it sure sounded like one to me."

Vicky continued, "All it said was that if Nibley didn't do something to help people get work, then he'd do whatever it takes to get him out of office."

Higgs reaffirmed, "Exactly, I told you that was a threat."

Vicky responded, "But Higgs, that could mean anything, even running against him in the next election."

Morty had to side with Vicky. "Well, if it is a threat, he didn't make it very clear."

Higgs countered, "Just sounds pretty suspicious to me. Pretty suspicious."

Morty added, "Well, I don't know what more Nibley can do."

"More than he's doing now," complained Higgs.

"Well, I've never seen a Mayor work harder, if you ask me," said Vicky. "He's usually up in his office until all hours of the night. And if he succeeds in putting away Big Jack and his boys, well then a lot of business men will have a lot more money to provide jobs for hard-working men and their families. I think Nibley's doing the right thing."

All Higgs could add was another, "Pretty suspicious."

After the conversation carried on for a short while longer, they decided to call it a night and said their good-byes on the sidewalk outside. Morty, the fatherly type that he was, once again brought up the topic Vicky hoped he'd avoid.

"Pretty young gal like you doesn't need to be hanging out with a couple of old-timers like us, Vicky. You should be out with some fellow."

That was the sore spot. And Higgs was smart enough to stay out of it. It was the only time he *never* voiced an opinion.

"Don't worry about me, Morty," Vicky reassured him and gave him a firm glare as she smiled through gritted teeth. "I'm just fine. Really I am."

The truth of it all was that there was no "fellow." Ever since she'd moved to Terminal City, Vicky had been focused on one thing: Getting a job on the crime beat. She didn't have time for romantic entanglements. Or at least that's what she told herself. And even if maybe she was a little lonely at times, it certainly didn't help to have Morty point it out to her.

"My wife could help you find somebody..."

Vicky quickly interrupted him and pushed him towards his car. "Good-night, Morty!"

As Morty drove off, Vicky realized that she had left her purse at City Hall. "Must still be in the press room."

Higgs offered to accompany her back over to retrieve it, but Vicky declined. "Don't worry, I'm a big girl. I'll be just fine on my own."

Higgs reluctantly agreed and Vicky walked the few short blocks back to City Hall. The walk was well-lit by street lamps and since Spring had finally arrived, it was a good night for a stroll. For a moment she regretted at least not getting a ride to save herself from the walk in heels. But that feeling quickly disappeared when she rounded the corner and found a crowd gathered outside the building, with two uniformed policemen guarding the main entrance. "What's going on?" she asked of the first person she encountered.

"Somebody heard gunshots in the building, then saw some big fellow rush out and jump into a car," answered a Gentleman in a three-piece-suit.

"Was anybody in the building?" Vicky asked.

"They think the Mayor was in there working late."

Vicky surveyed the upstairs windows of the four-story building. The Mayor's office was on the second floor, which was completely dark. "Well, his light's off," she pondered as she worked her way through the crowd towards the building entrance. The police were guarding the doors. Clearly, she wasn't going to get in that way. But if she could snatch a prize witness from a luxury hotel right under the nose of the Mob, a few Cops guarding a door couldn't stop her from getting in the very building where she spent most of her time.

Vicky walked around the dark side of the building to the window of the press room. It was still slightly open, just as they'd left it. She pushed the window up slowly and climbed right through. It was tricky in a skirt, but nothing she hadn't done before. Within minutes she was inside the building. She grabbed the camera she kept there, stuck a box of flash bulbs in her purse, and headed for the service stairwell. She knew the police would go up the main steps, and her best bet to avoid being spotted was to keep to the service route.

She was extra quiet climbing the stairs to the Mayor's

office just to be safe, but the closer she got to her destination, the more she was able to confirm that there was no one else in the building. Once she got within view, she could see that the door was open and the room was dark.

She peered in carefully and looked around. There was Nibley's body, face down in a pool of blood. There was no one else there. It was a disconcerting sight, looking at him. Seeing Dion O'Boyle was one thing — despite his kindness to her, he was still a ruthless gangster responsible for the deaths of who knew how many people. But Nibley was a good man who was fighting the good fight for the will of the people. And this is what he got for it.

Vicky lined up her first photo as best she could in the dark, then snapped it and used the light from the flash to position her next shot. In her haste to get as many photos as possible before anyone arrived, she burned her fingers trying to change the bulb. She quickly stuck her fingers in her mouth to cool them down then grabbed a handkerchief from her purse to handle the spent bulbs like the press photographers did. After she unscrewed it, she stopped for a second and wondered what to do with the thing. She could toss it into the trashcan, but that would leave clear evidence that she had been there. Her only choice was to drop it in her purse.

She grabbed her second shot and again used the light from the flash to line up her next angle before licking her fingers good, changing the bulb, and dropping the used one in her purse. She managed to get six (hopefully decent) shots before she ran out of bulbs. It was no matter. She heard footsteps coming down the hallway and was getting rather worried about the burning smell from her purse. She went for the doorway, but it was too late. She jumped behind the open door just as a gaggle of uniformed officers and detectives barged in.

CHAPTER FIVE

"WHO turned the light out?" barked Harry LaSalle, the Chief of Police. He was a no-nonsense man with a thick head of white hair and thick-rimmed glasses, and a man with whom Vicky had no desire to tangle.

"Cut the lights on!" shouted LaSalle. Vicky grabbed the opportunity to back out quietly as the detectives and officers fumbled in the dark for the switch.

She managed to duck out of the doorway just as the room lit up. The detectives were quick to note a set of footprints in the blood. "Look, Chief!" one shouted.

Vicky wanted to hear more, but couldn't take another risk at getting caught. Quickly and quietly, she headed back down the hall to the service stairwell.

Within minutes, she was back in the press room and out the window again. She took another look at the gathering crowd before jumping in her car to head back to the *Crusader* building. Frank would surely die from the story she was about to tell him. There would be quite a few "John-Brown-its!" shouted that night.

FRANK knew better to complain when his phone rang late at night. Betty certainly complained, but Frank knew better. "Red, what have you got?"

"A front page scoop! Nibley was murdered!"

"I'll be there in twenty minutes!" Frank shouted, barely hanging up the phone. He didn't bother with all of his clothing — just his pants and shoes, leaving his pajama top on. He couldn't wait to get the details. That was almost more exciting than getting the scoop itself.

It was actually less than twenty when Frank burst in through the doors of the Newsroom. It was a well-timed entrance as Vicky rushed out of the darkroom at the same time, clutching a handful of still soaking wet prints. "Frank, you got to see this!" she shouted to him.

She thrusted a dripping photo into his hands. There was Nibley, face down on the floor, dead as a doornail. It was a bit dark. Not the work of a crime-scene photographer, but certainly front-page worthy. "How did you get these?" Frank asked, reaching for the others.

"Not that," Vicky interrupted. "Look at his back."

Frank blinked a few times, still trying to adjust to the bright lights of the Newsroom and held the photo up close. "What am I looking for?" he finally had to ask.

Vicky jabbed at the picture with a slender finger. "Right there on the back of his shirt. Doesn't that look like somebody drew an 'X' on him? Probably in his own blood, too."

Frank moved the photo into better light. He studied it carefully for a few moments, then shook his head. "Maybe."

Vicky grabbed the photo from him and looked at it again. "You don't see it?"

Frank shrugged. "Might be something, Red. Hard to tell. Did you get any better ones?"

Vicky let out a deep sigh, "No. That's the best one. I was shooting in the dark. Literally."

Frank took another look. "Have Dan take a crack at it. He can blow it up, maybe get a better exposure."

"Yeah, okay," Vicky muttered as she sauntered off back to the darkroom.

VICKY'S photos were all over the front page the next morning, though they failed to mention the marking on Nibley's shirt. It was too faint to show up in newsprint, and Frank felt that if it could actually be a lead, they might want to keep it to themselves. Any advantage over the other papers in town was one worth keeping close to the vest. At least that's what he told Vicky.

Once again, thanks to her, the *Crusader* had the top scoop over every other paper in the city. This was the third time in as many months, and she felt certain that Frank would move her up to the crime beat. That was until she was called into his office to talk to the Police.

She and Frank were both escorted downtown to meet with the Chief of Police, Harry LaSalle. Vicky had narrowly avoided him the night before. But now, somehow, he knew all about how she'd managed to sneak through the window and up the back stairs. Vicky was puzzled. Had someone seen her?

LaSalle was irate and shouted at Vicky. "You stepped in the blood and left a trail of footprints all the way down to the press room. You disturbed a crime scene and made it that much more difficult for us to finger the killer!"

Vicky held her own. "Well, you may not know who the trigger man was, but if you want to know who was really responsible, you don't have to look any further than Big Jack!"

Frank tried to calm them down, knowing that they'd never get any information from the police if this was just a shouting match. "John Brown it, Red, the Chief is right, you did disturb a crime scene. I should fire you for that."

Vicky looked at him, surprised, but certainly knew better than to believe him. "You're right, I'm sorry. I'll clear out my desk when we get back." Vicky managed to produce a few sniffles, a hard swallow, and some fake tears.

"Now, Mr. Matson," consoled LaSalle, "I don't think we need to go that far." Just maybe she'd cracked that rough exterior. He wasn't used to dealing with gal reporters, after all.

"I'm so sorry," Vicky whimpered as she dabbed her eyes with a tissue.

Frank looked pensive in his feigned frustration, then softened and reassured her, "It's okay, Red. Just don't let it happen again."

"Thank you," she whispered, as Frank patted her hand before turning back to LaSalle.

"Sir, is there anything you can tell us about the crime? Do you have any leads?"

Vicky jumped in, "What about the mark on Nibley's shirt?"

LaSalle was wiser than they thought. "Nothing we can say right now. We'll let you know when we can. And Miss Rose?"

"Yes," Vicky said as she looked up.

"Be more careful where you step next time," added LaSalle. "Woman or not, I don't take kindly to reporters messing with my crime scenes, you got that?"

His expression said far more than his words.

IT WAS only a few days later when the Police announced that they had their man. Much to everyone's surprise, it wasn't one of Big Jack's men, but rather a regular family man and father of two, Harvey O'Donnell. Vicky recognized his name instantly from the dozens of "threatening" letters that he'd written to Nibley.

"Told you," said Higgs in the press room. "Told you it was suspicious. Pretty suspicious, I said. And I was right."

Vicky looked over the statement from the Chief. "I'll tell you what sounds suspicious, it's this statement."

"How so?" asked Morty. "They got a full confession. Even got the murder weapon with his fingerprints on it."

"But this fellow has no criminal record," challenged Vicky. "Never arrested for anything, not even spitting on the sidewalk. He's got a wife and two kids. So all of a sudden he's just so fed up that he kills the Mayor? I'm not buying it."

"Sounds like the case is closed to me," said Higgs. "The man confessed. What more do you want?"

"There's more going on here," said Vicky. "I don't know if the police even know it, but I promise you there is." She sat looking pensive, turning the details over and over in her mind.

"What about it?" asked Morty.

"Wouldn't you like to know?" Vicky answered with a grin. As much as she wanted to discuss the story with a friendly ear, she wasn't about to share it with someone from a competing paper.

THE NEXT day, when Harvey O'Donnell was arraigned, the courthouse was filled past capacity, the likes of which it had never seen. This was the first opportunity for Vicky and the other reporters to even see him. The Police had kept him under wraps, perhaps for his own protection, or perhaps for theirs. As Higgs would remark (more than once), it all sounded "pretty suspicious." This time, Vicky thought, Higgs was right.

As Vicky entered the press room, she got her first taste of what life would be like as a crime reporter. It started with a long wolf whistle and was followed by a thorough visual assessment and a final grunt of approval. It was the only approval she would receive as a "fellow crime reporter" for some time to come.

Vicky found herself face-to-face with her hoped-to-be rival newshounds, Charlie Hecht and Ben Gelbart of the *Terminal City Standard*. While Hecht's look was one of appreciation, even if for the completely wrong reasons, Gelbart's was clearly one of disdain.

"Hello, Boys," Vicky cooed to the tall, handsome and bespectacled Hecht. She knew the two by sight (and admittedly, with a little envy) and always thought Hecht looked more like a womanizing playwright than a newspaper reporter. Gelbart, the older and shorter of the two, took a long drag off of what was already his twelfth cigarette of the day and barked, "The Ladies' Room is down the hall, Sweetheart."

"What are you doing in here, Doll?" Hecht asked, cozying up to her. "This is where the big boys play."

She'd known it wouldn't be an easy welcome.

She also knew that politeness would get her nowhere. If she were going to play in their sandbox, she'd have to barrel in head first and scratch out her own turf, same as anyone else. Except in her case, she'd have to fight even harder.

"I'm here to cover the trial, same as you, Lampwick," Vicky asserted as she jumped right up into Hecht's face. "So, why don't the two of you back off and give me some space, you got it?" Then for good measure she shoved her way passed the two of them with such force that Gelbart dropped his butt.

"Out of my way, Smokestack!" she barked.

"Hey!" Gelbart shouted and quickly bent down to pick up his lost smoke.

Hecht's eyes were still on Vicky, though, and he let out another grunt of approval as she sauntered off and clacked her heels against the marble floor.

"Well, the company may not be much," Hecht mused, "but the scenery sure got a lot better."

A short time later, they were finally called to the courtroom for the hearing. As Vicky entered, she noticed a familiar, well-tailored presence in the back: Vito Spats Gennaro in his usual bowler hat and waxed moustache. He sat quietly in the very back and just watched. Vicky watched O'Donnell's expression as he was led in. He noticed Vito Spats, too.

The arrangement was a quick affair. O'Donnell, a pudgy, soft-spoken man with thinning hair, sat quietly before the Judge as the charge of murder was read. O'Donnell reasserted his confession and the Judge set the court date for the following month. There were no objections. It was all pretty cut and dry for a murder.

And as soon as it was over, Vito Spats left without saying a word.

As O'Donnell was led out into the hallway, Vicky and the other reporters got their only opportunity to shout their questions to him. "Why'd you do it? Do you think you'll hang? What about your family?" O'Donnell just kept walking with his head low until Vicky's question came to his ear. "Why'd you draw that mark on him?"

O'Donnell looked straight at her with a puzzled look on his face. Before he could speak, the Police whisked him around a corner and he disappeared into a sea of blue uniforms. For once, Higgs was definitely right.

Vicky had just reached for the handle on her car door outside in the parking lot when she sensed a tall shadow approach from behind her. Her breath went short and her pulse jumped as she quickly pulled on the door with hope of getting inside. Her heart skipped a beat when a muscular hand reached out quickly and grabbed the door, forcing it to a sudden stop. She wheeled around quickly to face the expected bowler hat and waxed moustache, but was surprised and quite relieved to see Charlie Hecht tower over her instead.

"What was that all about?" he asked with a light chuckle as he shook his head.

Vicky hesitated to answer, careful to think over her words and not give anything away to her competition. She needn't have bothered.

"Listen," he told her as he took her hand and caressed it gently. Then he continued in his easy-going and seductive drawl, "I've got nothing against girl reporters. I think there should be more of you. I'm even willing to help you out. Tell you what, let me take you out to dinner and I'll show you the ropes. Tell you everything I know about the news business. What do you say, Sweetheart?"

It was a tone that had surely sent many a woman to swoon and fall to his every whim.

But not her.

Yes, she was tempted and could see the attraction — there was the physical attraction, of course. And it would have been the perfect opportunity to size up her competition, on his dime no less.

But she was smart enough to see what he was up to. He may not have been as straightforward and belligerent as Gelbart, but his aims were no different.

"No, thanks, Abercrombie," she told him flatly, then jerked her car door open. She hopped right in and drove straight off.

Lost in the fanfare of O'Donnell's court appearance was the fact that Councilman Eugene Barker, Tackman's right-hand man, "reluctantly and with great sadness" stepped up to fulfill the rest of Nibley's term as Mayor, which was to say the majority of it. And with that, the biggest news of all didn't appear in a single headline — Big Jack had regained control of the Mayor's office. The status quo had returned.

CHAPTER SIX

WHEN Vicky got back to the office, she went straight to Frank to give him the full scoop, though she left out her second run-in with Hecht. She was careful to relate her tale with building excitement and she finally reached the grand climax — that O'Donnell didn't know what she was talking about when she asked him about the mark on Nibley's shirt!

Frank just sat back and shook his head, "John Brown." Frank had as good an ear for news as any reporter alive, but even he thought she might be reaching on this one. "Red, I know there were a dozen reporters all shouting questions at the fellow. How do you even know he was responding to you?"

"Because he didn't respond to anyone else, and he looked straight at me," Vicky answered.

"Then he probably couldn't understand you," Frank replied. "There was just too much going on."

Vicky replied, "Maybe so, but I still want to do some checking. There's just something about this thing that keeps nagging at me, and I want to find out what it is."

Frank told her, "Okay, you can check all you want, but it better not interfere with your regular work. Remember, you're still on the City Hall beat. Just because you landed a few hot stories, doesn't mean I'm moving you up."

VICKY went straight down to the basement, to "the morgue," as the reporters referred to it, where all the back stories were stored and catalogued. She ventured inside and found herself in a maze of filing cabinets and piles of newspapers still left to be clipped and sorted. There was a tiny desk in the corner, barely visible under stacks of files. The name plate on the desk read, "Denny Morris."

"Hello?" she called out.

"Hello," came an answer from the back, and with that a tall, gangly, sort-of-handsome fellow (well, with a little polish), peered out from the cabinets in the rear. He weaved his way quickly to the front, delighted to see Vicky.

He courteously extended a hand to shake as she introduced herself and wasted no time in getting straight to the point. "I could use some help. I'm trying to find something, but I'm not sure what it is."

"I'll be glad to help all I can. Which editor is this for?" Denny asked.

Vicky stopped for a moment then realized what he meant. "I'm not a secretary, Mr. Morris. I'm a reporter."

Denny tossed his head back at the realization, quickly apologizing as he moved to a particular cabinet. "So sorry. Is this a society column?"

"No," Vicky asserted through gritted teeth. "Believe it or not, I'm a real, honest-to-goodness reporter."

Denny stepped back into the comfort of his filing cabinets. "Maybe if you just told me what you're looking for?" he offered.

"Right," she told him, keeping her tongue in check. She wasn't about to let her own irritation get in the way of chasing this story. "Do you know of any previous murder where the killer marked his victim with an 'X'? Probably drawn in the victim's blood?"

"Ah," Denny lit up, sensing a chance to chime in without stepping on her toes. "The Nibley case."

Vicky looked at him with surprise. "You know about that?"

"Of course," Denny answered, puzzled by her surprise. "I filed all the photos."

"Right," Vicky answered as the realization sunk in.

"I thought that sounded familiar, too," Denny continued. He paused for a moment, then looked at his watch.

"Is there a problem?" she asked.

"Well, actually, I was about to leave to go get some dinner with the folks. But you're welcome to look through the files all you want." He pointed to a long wall full of filing cabinets. "That's the murder section over there. I'm afraid there's quite a lot of them."

"Well, don't worry about me," Vicky assured him. "I'm a big girl. I'll be just fine."

"Good night, then." Denny would have tipped his hat if he'd had one. Instead, he just sort of half-way bowed, not knowing what else to do, as he backed his way out of the door. Vicky went straight to the files and pulled open the first drawer.

A FEW hours later, Denny returned to find her still at it, sleepy-eyed, but not giving up. "Thought I'd find you still here," he said, and placed a tightly-wrapped paper bag on the desk in front of her.

"What's this?" she asked.

"Brought you some dinner," he replied. "Courtesy of mother's fine home cooking. Figured you'd be hungry. Figured I owed it to you, too."

"Oh, don't worry about that," Vicky assured him as she opened the bag. "I get that all the time. Works to my advantage sometimes, too. Believe me."

She looked back at him and saw a different person than the one she'd met just a few hours before. "Thank you."

Vicky opened the bag and took in the smell of roast beef, potatoes, carrots, and bread that made her mouth water. There was even a fork and a napkin. She hadn't realized just how hungry she was.

Denny sat quietly across from her, watching her eat. At first she thought he was just ogling her, but then she noticed the wheels were turning inside his head.

"Did you want to ask me something?" she queried.

Denny looked away and stammered, "Well, actually, if you don't think I'm being too forward. I was just wondering how you got to be a reporter."

"So, how does a woman get to be a reporter?" she asked in between bites. "It's killing you, isn't it?"

Denny tried to deny it, but it was no use. He wasn't any good at poker, either.

"All right," she told him, "since you brought me dinner, I'll give you the quick version."

Surprised, Denny sat up in his chair, listening intently. Vicky detailed how she grew up in Missouri, went to college at the University, and had fully intended to become a school teacher. "That's what every other gal in my family did before they got married and had a bunch of kids. While I was in college, though, I was always strapped for cash, so I managed to wrangle myself a job working as an assistant editor for the college paper. To this day, I still don't know how I lied my way into that one."

Grabbing another bite, Vicky continued. The more she got into her story, the less lady-like she ate. "That's when I got the bug. Wanted to become a reporter, I mean. My family hated the idea, especially my father. So, like any good little girl, I did what Daddy wanted and became a school teacher."

Denny couldn't help but think how none of his teachers ever looked a thing like her. Too bad he didn't grow up in Missouri.

"But after about two years," Vicky told him, licking her fork clean, "I just couldn't take it any more. So I marched myself down to the city editor at the *Southeast Missourian* and tried to lie my way into another job. At least this time I was more qualified."

"So, that's how you got started?" Denny asked.

"Not a chance. Turned me down flat," she replied. "Said he didn't need a gal reporter, nor did he want one. So, I got a job as a clerk at a nearby hotel, which worked out great, because I got to meet a lot of people and learned all kinds of stuff that went on in town. Then every week, I went back to see that editor until I finally wore him down. I think he hired me just to get me off his back. He was pretty glad when I finally quit and moved up here."

Vicky crumpled the empty bag and tossed it into the trashcan. "So, now that I've spilled my guts, what's your story?"

Denny shook his head. "Certainly nothing as interesting

as yours. Born here, grew up here. Went to college, got a job in the library." Denny motioned to the cabinets and shelves surrounding him. "Still working in the library, more or less."

"Ever thought about doing something else?"

Denny hopped to his feet and turned to the filing cabinets. "So how far did we get?"

Vicky didn't have to be an ace reporter to know that the subject had most definitely been changed.

"Oh, you don't have to help me. I can manage just fine."

"Can't leave you in here all night by yourself. With two people on the job, we'll get done a whole lot quicker," he told her.

She couldn't argue with that.

CHAPTER SEVEN

THE SUN was nearly up before Denny uttered the words both of them had been waiting all night to hear. "Found it."

Vicky sat up, sleepy-eyed, having dozed off with a folder sitting in her lap.

Denny scanned the article and reeled off the details to her. "Fifteen years ago. District Attorney Thomas Gregor. He'd been trying to take down Big Jack. Murdered in his own home. Killer was a thug named "Three-Finger" Ned Vogel. He also shot their young boy, Brent. And the Mother. Just before he escaped, Three-Finger Ned dipped his finger in Gregor's blood and drew an 'X' on the back of his shirt!" Denny felt pretty good about himself.

Spurred on by this information, Vicky and Denny dug through the rest of the file and the subsequent articles. Three-Finger Ned had been caught a few days later. At his trial, he was deemed insane and sentenced to the local asylum. Mrs. Gregor never recovered from her wounds or her grief and died some ten years later at the same asylum. Young Brent Gregor was confined to a wheelchair and still lived in the Gregor mansion. He'd been romantically linked with socialite and famed female pilot Abigail Wentworth for a time, but otherwise had largely remained a recluse.

They both sat back in relief. They'd found what they were looking for, and it went deeper than either of them suspected. Well, more than Denny expected. It all started to make just a little more sense.

The sun was coming up and Vicky needed to be at work

soon, back on the City Hall beat once again, as Frank had asserted.

"Would you mind going out for some breakfast?" Denny asked.

"Afraid I can't," Vicky answered as she threw her shoes back on and grabbed the file. "Mind if I hang on to this?" Before Denny could answer, she blurted out, "I've got just enough time to run home and freshen up before I have to be back in the office. Maybe a rain check?"

And with that, she was out the door. The disheveled files and the scent of her perfume were the only reminders of their long night together.

VICKY bolted straight into Frank's office and laid it out for him. She didn't let him get a single word in before she was through. All he could do is drop his proofs and listen.

"John Brown it, Red. You're crazy. The man confessed. His fingerprints are on the weapon. All *five* of them. Maybe this 'Three-Finger Ned' drew an 'X' on his victim. So what? It doesn't prove a thing. That was over ten years ago!"

"Well, I still want to follow up on it. I think there's something to it, and it'll just keep nagging at me if I don't," Vicky told him. No matter what he said, he knew she'd keep digging at it anyway.

"And it was fifteen," she corrected him.

"So, what's your plan?" he asked, as he scratched his stubbled chin. Frank skipped shaving so often, Vicky wondered why he didn't just grow a beard.

"There's one witness to the Gregor murder who's still alive. The son, Brent Gregor. I'll just go talk to him and see what I can find out."

Frank sat back in his chair, chuckling. "Then you might as well give up now, because you'll never get in there. Brent Gregor is a recluse. He just sits in his wheelchair all day, staring out the window. He doesn't go anywhere, and he sure as heck doesn't see anybody. I hear that old place is haunted anyway."

Vicky answered sharply, "Well, if there's one thing that John Nibley taught me, it's that you won't get anywhere if you don't try."

"Yeah," Frank retorted, "and you see where it got him."

Vicky wasn't about to let this observation dampen her enthusiasm. "Well, I'm just glad to finally be on the crime beat," she retorted as she spun around for the door.

But Frank's reply stopped her dead in her tracks. "You're not on the crime beat, Red. Nibley may have been murdered, but he was also the Mayor. Technically, this is still a City Hall story. And you're headed right back there as soon as you're done chasing this one around."

Vicky looked at him sharply, unable to think of anything to say that wouldn't get her fired on the spot. All she could do is let her heels clack extra loud all the way down the hall as she stormed out.

MAYOR NIBLEY'S murder and the events that followed, ending with O'Donnell's arrest, brought a brief respite to the Mob war. Many incorrectly guessed that the Mayor's death had actually brought an end to the violence, since he had been on such a crusade to put an end to the Mob's influence in city politics. A few even went so far as to believe that Nibley's death had actually been "good for the city" since his absence seemed to usher in a new era of peace and tranquility that had so far lasted almost two weeks.

They couldn't have been more wrong.

The unplanned and unofficial "cease fire" between the South and North Side mobs was summarily shattered the next morning after Vicky had set her sights on visiting Brent Gregor.

Vito Spats Gennaro stood at the window of his luxurious suite at the Belmont Hotel and enjoyed his morning cup of coffee. It was a beautiful spring morning outside and the early sun bathed everything he saw in a golden sheen. The only thing more beautiful was his lovely dark-haired wife, Annette, as she slinked into the room adorned in the skimpiest of her white negligee. She hugged him from behind and rested her head on his strong back.

"Do you have to leave so early?" she asked in her cooing voice that he was oftentimes powerless to resist.

"I'm afraid so," he answered as he turned around to take her in his arms and slip his large hands around her slender waist. He stared down into her beautiful, child-like brown eyes. She was nearly twenty years younger than he, barely more than a child in comparison. But she'd been exactly what he needed to help him forget the pain of losing his first wife, Rosa, to colitis. His dear Rosa had died in his arms just two years before. He needed someone young and vibrant to help him erase that crushing memory. Someone who would stay that way for a long time to come.

"Big Jack is waiting for me," he told her, then gave her a lingering kiss before he headed for the door. As part of his daily routine, he checked with his men in the hallway before giving Annette one last kiss good-bye, then left their suite and made certain to shut the door firmly behind him. His men gave each other a sly nod, knowing that the young Mrs. was barely dressed and alone inside for the better part of the day. But a sly nod was all it was, because they knew better than to even think of taking advantage of the situation.

Vito Spats took the elevator down to the ornate lobby lit with a dozen crystal chandeliers. After another check with his men at the front windows, he greeted the golden morning sun in person as the Hotel Doorman opened the large glass and iron door and bid him a good day.

Vito gave a quick glance outside and acknowledged the nod from his driver, "Cherry Nose" Caifano, newly returned from Miami. Cherry Nose held open the door of Vito's black four-door touring sedan then quickly shut it as the boss climbed inside. Leaving his hotel was a precision operation that went down like clockwork each and every morning.

It was a quiet drive for the first two blocks. The rest of the city was busy at work and there was very little traffic. But Cherry Nose knew his job well and grew quite suspicious of the curtained black sedan that seemed to follow in the distance. After Big Jack's narrow escape just a few weeks before, Cherry Nose knew that he couldn't be too careful.

"Looks like we got somebody, Boss," Cherry Nose alerted Vito Spats as he hit the gas. "Better duck down."

Vito Spats turned sharply in his seat just as the car behind them accelerated suddenly in a bold attempted to overtake them. It was clearly a repeat of the attack on

Big Jack. Spats ducked low and drew his pistol. Cherry Nose did the same and held firm on the gas to reach top speed. The car behind them sped up as well, its occupants determined not to lose the chase.

Cherry Nose shouted for Spats to hang on just as he whipped the steering wheel and the car slid around a corner like a dog running across a tile floor.

Cherry Nose hit the gas again as the tires caught the pavement. The car surged forward and bolted down the street, narrowly missing a line of cars parked on the curb.

Their would-be attackers nearly lost control when they attempted the same turn, but the driver was more skilled than Cherry Nose hoped he would be and managed to stay in the chase.

Cherry Nose gunned the engine for all it was worth and zigged by two passing cars in the opposite lane, but it was soon clear that the pursuing vehicle was easily the faster of the two.

"No luck, Boss!" Cherry Nose alerted Spats.

Never one to wait for a fight, Vito Spats leaned out the window and fired off several rounds. He took out a headlight and a portion of the windshield (not to mention the tail light of another passing car), but it wasn't enough to slow their attackers down.

"Faster! Faster!" Vito ordered.

"I got it all the way to the floor!" Cherry Nose countered as he spend around another corner.

Spats leaned back out and fired at the car again, but a bump against the curb caused most of his volleys to miss their mark.

Spats shouted for Cherry Nose to duck when he saw two Tommy guns emerge from the car. He just managed to dive for the floorboards when a hail of bullets struck their speeding vehicle from behind and shattered all of the windows around him.

Spats peered up for just a second when the shooting stopped and wondered if Cherry Nose had survived.

"You okay, Boss?" Cherry Nose shouted, confirming that he was alive and still tucked behind the wheel.

Before he could answer, Spats felt himself being flung

sideways into the floor as Cherry Nose whipped the wheel again and they careened around another turn.

This latest move was greeted with the sound of squealing tires and more gunfire from behind them. Spats and Cherry Nose both ducked down again as their car received another vicious pounding of screeching lead.

Spats reloaded his pistol and waited for the rain of bullets to stop. Just as soon as it did, he sat straight up and blasted back at them through the rear window. He wished on the Sacred Mother that he'd been armed with more than a hand gun. It was a mistake he promised himself he would never make again.

Cherry Nose gunned the engine once more, but he'd turned down a long avenue with no easy escape. Their only hope was to outrun or out-blast their opponents, and neither scenario was very likely, considering what had already transpired.

Their enemies quickly gained speed and, getting a break in the oncoming traffic, moved right up alongside them. Cherry Nose swerved to the side in a vain attempt to keep away, but the road simply wasn't wide enough for that to be the least bit effective. Spats fired again at the car and managed to hit one of the gunmen in the back seat.

It was then that he got a good look at Whitey O'Leary just as his dread rival raised his Tommy gun once more to empty another burning host of rounds into their vehicle.

Cherry Nose took the only action available and slammed right into the car with a jerk of his steering wheel. Whitey was knocked off balance and fell backwards into the seat.

Cherry Nose grabbed the chance in a mad hope to make it to the next turn, but a final blast of gunfire from Whitey struck their back wheel and sent them careening out of control.

Cherry Nose only managed to shout something unintelligible before their car slid sideways off the road and smashed broadside into a nearby brick building. He and Spats were both thrown headlong into the floorboards and showered with bits of glass and crumpled metal.

CHAPTER EIGHT

VITO SPATS was momentarily stunned as he lay in the floor of the vehicle and stared at the bullet-shredded ceiling above him. He could hear Whitey's vehicle screech to a halt nearby.

Then came the sounds of car doors being opened. And multiple footsteps as they raced toward him.

He was sure he would die.

"Cherry Nose?" Spats called out as he reached for his pistol. It was nowhere to be found.

Everything was silent except for the footsteps. And Spats' own heartbeat.

Both of which grew ever closer.

The silence was shattered by another blast of gunfire.

Only it wasn't from a Tommy gun.

And it hadn't come from their assailants.

Vito Spats looked up to see his driver's bloodied face lean over the car seat above him. Cherry Nose's outstretched arm blasted away until another return spray silenced him.

Spats tried to scurry out of the wreckage as the footsteps came for him again, but it was no use.

The car door was flung open and two firm hands grabbed Vito by the lapels. They drug him out of the car in one clean jerk. In the next second, the still-stunned Vito Spats found himself lying face up on the gritty pavement as Whitey and two others stood over him with the smoking barrels of their Tommy guns.

This time, he would surely die.

"Been waiting a long time for this," Whitey chuckled as he stuck the red-hot barrel of his machine gun into Vito's face. Vito just stared back with fiery, piercing eyes. He would stare down his killer to the very end.

But the weapon of death clicked on an empty chamber.

Whitey swore over his breath and pulled the trigger again and again.

Frustrated, he angrily thrust the machine gun into one of his fellow assassin's hands as sirens filled the air from a short distance away.

"I'm empty, Boss," the gunman told Whitey.

Whitey turned to his other accomplice and got the same response.

"You lucky son-of-a-dog!" Whitey laughed at Spats. He quickly cleared his throat and spat in Vito's face. The saliva ran down Spats' cheek and mixed with his blood.

Whitey and the two others raced back to their car and quickly sped away.

It seemed like it was only seconds before three police cruisers screeched to a halt in the street from both directions.

Vito Spats chuckled to himself. He'd never thought he would be glad to see the police. He probably still wasn't, but the irony of it all hadn't escaped him.

When he stopped laughing to himself, he was puzzled to discover that he could still hear his chuckles echo through the air.

Then he realized that it wasn't him laughing at all.

It was Cherry Nose.

He'd taken seven bullets and was still alive. That's why he drove for Vito Spats.

AFTER a few days' worth of planning, Vicky pulled her small car into the huge driveway of the Gregor Mansion and stopped for a long moment to take in the dark, imposing house. It looked more like a fortress, completely gated, with bars on the doors and windows and Guards posted all around. Had she seen it fifteen years earlier, she would have instantly remarked at how much it had changed from an opulent, welcoming castle to the dungeon that it had become. It certainly looked haunted, too. No wonder they call it *The Murder Mansion*, she thought.

Vicky approached the front door and spoke with the Guards. They looked down on her to assert their dominion. They needn't have worried. Just their appearance alone made her question the wisdom of this visit.

"I just need to speak to the Master of the House, if you don't mind," she said, her voice shaking slightly. They looked her over and quickly sensing that she was no threat, stepped aside.

"Knock," was the only word that either of them would utter.

Vicky rapped the large door knocker and waited for what seemed an eternity. Eventually, the grand door squeaked open, but only just a few inches. A portly, genteel Englishman, his graying hair combed perfectly back, his neatly trimmed beard flecked with white, peered at her through the doorway. She guessed correctly that this was Bernard Worthington, Brent Gregor's personal valet, as had been described in the numerous articles contained in the file folder she had taken from Denny.

Vicky politely introduced herself as a "journalist" from the *Daily Crusader* (the word "reporter" just seemed completely inappropriate in such surroundings), and stated that she wished to see Mr. Gregor.

Worthington answered quickly in his kind, melodic voice, "Master Gregor will see no one. Least of all the Press."

Before she could utter another word, the door was shut and the Guards stepped back into position. Frank was right. Getting in to see Gregor was impossible.

Frustrated, Vicky went back to the newspaper. As she reached the stairwell, rather than go upstairs to tell Frank that he had been correct, she opted to head back downstairs to the morgue.

She found Denny asleep in his office. "This what they pay you to do?" she asked, startling him awake. Denny sat straight up, knocking over the stack of files that he'd been working on.

"Vicky," was all he managed to blurt out, pleasantly surprised.

"That offer for breakfast still open?" she asked.

Denny looked at his watch and struggled to focus. "I'm afraid breakfast is over. But how about lunch?"

"Yeah, that'll do," she snapped back.

Denny took her to the Cosmic Café, a cozy little eatery that he frequented, as did many of the staff at the *Crusader*. Vicky had rarely been there herself, since she spent most of her time camped out at City Hall. She waved to a few of her co-workers who wondered who was the gangly fellow with whom she was lunching. None of them knew that he was a co-worker, too.

Denny watched wide-eyed as she downed a double chocolate malt with her sandwich and then asked for another.

While they ate, Vicky told Denny all about her disastrous visit to the Gregor mansion. He sat up with interest, wanting to know what it was really like. "I've only seen photographs of it in the paper. I heard it's haunted."

"Looks haunted, too," Vicky assured him. "Not that I ever want to go back there, but I think if I could just talk to Mr. Gregor, I might be able to get somewhere with this story. But no one can see him. The butler barely even opened the door to talk to me."

"Not 'no one,'" Denny told her, shaking his head and smiling. "There is one person who sees him. Twice a week, in fact. His nurse."

"Oh?" Vicky asked. "How do you know this?"

"The paper," Denny replied. "You should try reading it sometime, instead of just writing it."

She'd heard those words before.

DISGUISING herself as a nurse turned out to be harder than Vicky expected. She easily looked the part and had no problem paying off Brent Gregor's regular nurse for the opportunity, but it was learning the procedures that she would have to convincingly perform that reminded her of why she hadn't gone to nursing school in the first place. Too bad he didn't need a school teacher. That she could have done easily.

Since she'd been there only a few days before, she donned a blonde wig to go with her uniform. She certainly liked the flat, comfortable shoes and gave some thought to wearing them on the job herself.

She didn't really get nervous until she reached the end of the driveway and looked up at the imposing house. The Guards stood firm and menacingly at their positions. She thought about turning back, but she had gotten this far and it didn't make sense to not at least try. What was the worst that could happen? she thought. It wasn't like she was trying to con her way into seeing Big Jack. She'd already done that before, or at least something close to it.

As Vicky reached the front door, the Guards dutifully stepped aside. Of course, she realized, they were expecting her. She knocked at the door and waited for another eternity. It was unnerving standing between the Guards, but when she glanced up at them, neither seemed to be scrutinizing her.

Finally, the great door swung open, this time all the way. It was Bernard Worthington again, and he stepped aside in gentlemanly fashion to let her in. She'd had the regular nurse call ahead to say that she was ill and was sending a replacement in her stead. It seemed to have worked. Worthington gave a quick instruction, "Follow me, please," and led her upstairs.

Vicky stopped to quickly take in the interior view. Beside the staircase was a dull suit of armor brandishing a mace in one hand. Some other weapon appeared to be missing from the other. The great house looked even larger on the inside than it did on the outside. Vicky stared in wide-eyed amazement as they climbed the winding staircase to the second floor. Forget The Lexington, this was the place to be. The ceilings were high enough to fit two or more floors of The Lexington easily.

Worthington led her down a vast, luxurious hallway to the room at the far end. If it was all meant to impress and impose upon the casual visitor, it worked. For a night in this place, she didn't care what Gregor looked like. Or that he was in a wheelchair.

Worthington quietly opened the door and led her inside. The Master Bedroom was large but plainly decorated. A four-poster bed sat at the far end of the room, covered with simple blankets. There were no pictures, and most every surface of the dressers and tables were covered with stacks of books.

There in a wheelchair, sitting with an open novel on his covered lap was a strikingly handsome man, though very pale and stern. So, this was Brent Gregor. Vicky couldn't help but feel sorry for him after having read about that horrible night so many years ago. The thoughts quickly took her mind away from the opulent surroundings.

"Master Gregor," Worthington intoned, "the Nurse is here."

Brent Gregor gave a quick hand motion, which obviously meant to show her in and let her get to work. He didn't bother to look up at her. He just closed his book and stared out the window.

"Don't hesitate to call if you need any assistance," Worthington told her as he left the room.

Vicky opened her bag and quickly rehearsed everything in her mind as she knelt down next to him. She tried to look at his face, but he kept his gaze on the window and paid her no mind. She surmised that he'd been through this process so many times that he'd probably rather just sleep through it all.

She took his blood pressure and despite a few minor errors, felt that she'd managed to pull that off without a hitch. He instinctively unbuttoned his shirt, still without looking at her. "Beautiful day out to-day, isn't it?" she asked as she listened to his heartbeat. He seemed to mumble an answer, then dutifully breathed in and out when she asked him.

Then it came time for his injection. This was the part that Vicky was least sure about, despite several rehearsals with various pieces of fruit. She said, "Terrible shame about the Mayor," as she prepared the needle, then remembered that she was supposed to apply the tourniquet first.

Brent Gregor looked back at her as she attempted to set the needle on the edge of her bag. "The Mayor?" he asked as she reached up to tie the rubber hose around his arm.

"Yes," she responded. "I thought it was really strange how the killer drew an 'X' on him. It reminded me of another —"

Brent Gregor jerked away before she could finish her sentence and wheeled over to a small table. Vicky stood up as he rang his bell loudly.

"Please," she begged. "I need your help! An innocent man could be executed!"

Brent Gregor rang his bell even louder, calling out. "Worthington! Worthington!"

Within seconds, Worthington rushed into the room. "Worthington, this woman is an imposter! Escort her from the property at once!"

"Yes, Sir!" he answered, taking Vicky by the arm.

She made one last attempt as Worthington led her to the door. "Please, Mr. Gregor. My name is Vicky Rose. I'm a reporter for the *Daily Crusader*. I need your help to serve justice. Please, won't you help me?"

Brent raised his hand for them to stop, then glared at her. "I tried to serve justice once before, and *this* is where it got me!" He slammed his fist on the armrest. With that, he turned his wheelchair around, back towards the window.

Worthington didn't have to lead her back out. She was two steps ahead of him. He could barely keep up with her as she marched down the hallway and back down the stairs.

When they reached the front door, Vicky apologized for her deception. "I can understand if you wish to press charges against me, but I ask that you please take pity on your usual nurse. She only did this to help. I'm trying to save an innocent man's life."

Worthington said, "We would rather avoid the publicity of pressing charges, but I'm afraid the nurse will have to be discharged."

Vicky, hanging her head in regret, apologized again. "Thank you for your kindness."

Worthington, ever the gentleman, replied, "Perhaps we shall meet again under better circumstances. Good day, Miss."

AFTER getting out of her nurse uniform, Vicky went straight to the morgue to tell Denny about her second fiasco at the Gregor Mansion. She'd had so many successes lately, she was starting to think that someone was watching over her. Perhaps that was true, and it was time for her to come down a few pegs.

"Did you see any ghosts?" Denny asked her.

"Only the owner," Vicky answered. It didn't take him long to figure out I wasn't a real nurse. I was obviously barking up the wrong tree. The only thing I managed to do was get his regular nurse fired. Now I'm just at a dead end, since Gregor was the only witness who's still alive."

"No, as I recall, there was another witness," Denny added.

"Who?" asked Vicky, puzzled.

"Three-Finger Ned," chimed Denny. "I've been doing some more research for you. Ned is still an inmate at the asylum." Denny handed her a brand new file. Vicky sat up in interest. Things were suddenly looking not so bleak after all.

Vicky skimmed through the file, then looked back at him, curious. "Why are you doing all this?"

"Doing what?" Denny asked, looking away.

"You know, all this extra research," she said, trying to look him in the eye. He turned away quickly and went back to another stack of files.

Vicky followed and her reporter instincts kicked in. She could always tell when someone was avoiding the truth. Perhaps this wasn't the best time to exercise that particular skill, but sometimes she just couldn't help herself.

"Surely you have other work to do," she prodded.

Denny acted surprised that she even had to ask, but was still unable to look her in the eye. "You think I enjoy being stuck down here in the morgue day after day?"

She nodded in agreement.

"I've been working on these files for a couple of years now," he added, more confident. It's great to finally be able to put some of my efforts to use."

Now she was getting somewhere. "So, if you weren't working down here every day, what else would you be doing?" she asked.

His confidence quickly deflated. "I don't know. Just something else."

"Like what?" she asked.

Denny went for his previous tactic of quickly changing the subject, but this time he really surprised her when he blurted out, "I know what can cheer you up. What do say we go out and get some dinner? I know a great little Italian place."

Dinner wasn't at all what she'd had in mind. It was something tall, cold, and full of chocolate. Then her eyes lit up, seeing the full picture. "Oh, I get it now. So, that's why you're helping me."

"No," Denny backtracked, "not at all." He stumbled on his words and fell back into a filing cabinet.

"You sure?" she asked him coyly, using much the same look she'd used on the Busboy at the Lexington. It was great for getting information.

"No," Denny replied, picking up the files he'd knocked down. "I, uh, just thought it'd be nice to go to dinner, that's all."

Vicky was quick to respond, "Well, I appreciate the invitation, but if you were asking me on a date, I'm afraid I just don't have time in my life for romance right now. Please don't take it the wrong way."

Denny shrugged, "Don't worry, I understand. Really." His expression, however, said otherwise. "I just want to help."

Vicky eyed him suspiciously. It was true, she couldn't have gotten nearly as far as she had without his assistance.

"Okay," she told him. "Helper it is then."

LATER that night, as she walked into her quiet apartment, she took a long, slow look around. For some reason, it seemed rather empty for a change. Denny was a nice enough man, but she didn't have time in her life for romantic entanglements. She was too focused on her career. Far too much to do there.

She shrugged off whatever it was she was feeling. As she walked to the bedroom, something caught her attention out of the corner of her eye. There on a chair by the window was a book. She didn't remember leaving it there, but it didn't matter. She was immediately struck by the thought of one person. Brent Gregor. So alone up in the large mansion of his.

But that wasn't her.

That wasn't her at all.

CHAPTER NINE

VICKY stopped her car at the front gate of the Terminal City Asylum and anxiously waited for the Guard to motion her in. It had taken nearly a week for her to break away from the City Hall beat, and she was excited to finally be there, even if it was only temporary and just for one story. The entire grounds were encompassed by a tall, wrought iron fence with barbed wire woven between the top spikes.

As she pulled up the drive, the trees broke to provide a full view of the asylum. It was a large, red brick castle-like conglomeration of multiple buildings built end to end and connected at the corners. In the very center, which was the entrance, was a tall, narrow spire that appeared to be a bell tower. The collection of high-pitched rooftops gave it a rather jagged appearance. The windows and doors were all covered with iron bars or sealed off entirely. It was much larger than the Gregor Mansion, and certainly far more imposing.

Vicky parked her car by the front door and went inside.

She stopped at the front Nurse's desk and told them of her appointment. The Nurse asked her to wait, saying that Dr. Hyneman would be with her shortly. Vicky took in her surroundings — gleaming tile floors, nondescript white walls. While the outside looked like a prison, the inside looked like a hospital. It smelled like one, too.

Before she could sit down, she was greeted by a slight, kindly man with a bushy grey goatee and a mild German accent. Just what she expected.

"Miss Rose, I presume?" he asked.

"Yes," she smiled, "Dr. Hyneman, so wonderful to meet you. I can't tell you how much I appreciate your allowing me to visit."

Vicky quickly explained that she was researching some old stories, and wanted to check on the progress of Ned Vogel.

"Yes, he's one of our oldest patients," Dr. Hyneman told her. "He's been with us for almost fifteen years now. Would you like to see him?"

"Of course," answered Vicky, impressed with his candor.

"Follow me, then," replied Dr. Hyneman. "Right this way." He led her down the left hallway to the elevator. They went up two floors, then down several more halls past bathrobed patients who wandered silently and aimlessly. The overhead lights were dim, providing a peaceful counterbalance to the occasional screams that echoed from further down the halls.

Eventually, they reached a room that had "Vogel" posted on the outside door. The door was fitted with a window that allowed them to peer inside. "Don't worry," Dr. Hyneman assured her, "he can't see us. It is just a mirror on the other side."

Vicky watched Ned through the glass. She immediately recognized him from his newspaper photos, though he was certainly older, grayer, and with slightly less hair. He just sat rocking back and forth in his chair, staring off into space. She looked at his large hands on the arms of the rockers, taking note of his right hand, which was missing the last two fingers.

"As you can see," Dr. Hyneman finally intoned, "Mr. Vogel lives in a world of his own making. I'm afraid he won't be leaving us anytime soon."

After observing Ned for some time, watching him just rock back and forth, keeping regular time like a metronome, Dr. Hyneman led Vicky back to his office.

"Well," Vicky pondered, "after seeing Mr. Vogel for myself, it certainly seems silly of me to have come up here. Still, I appreciate your patience and your time."

"Quite all right," Dr. Hyneman reassured her. "We get

few visitors, so as you can imagine, a kind and pretty face is always welcome here." He smiled at her warmly. She could read the appreciation of her visit in his eyes.

"Why, thank you," Vicky replied. "If I could ask just one more question, though?"

"Certainly," Dr. Hyneman answered.

"When Mr. Vogel killed Thomas Gregor, he marked him with an 'X'. Do you know why that was?" she asked with a puzzled look.

"Ah yes," Dr. Hyneman's face lit up. "I found that very curious myself. The Gregor murder is not the only one where he marked the victim. There were several previous instances."

"Oh?" Vicky responded with surprise.

"My colleagues theorized," Dr. Hyneman continued, "that Mr. Vogel used it as a Mark of Death. A ritualistic symbol, if you will. But the actual reason is much more simple." He paced around his desk, rolling the thoughts over in his mind.

"Oh," she asked, following him with her eyes.

"Yes. You see, Mr. Vogel is illiterate. He was just leaving his mark. Like an artist signing his work."

"I see," Vicky replied, "interesting." Rather interesting indeed, she thought, though she wasn't sure what she could actually do with the information.

As Dr. Hyneman led her back to the front, she shook his hand gently and thanked him for his time.

VICKY may not have had any romantic notions about Denny, but he was quickly becoming her go-to guy for lamenting her lack of progress. Perhaps it was because her usual sounding board, Frank, felt that there was no story to uncover, and Denny was a willing and friendly ear. She was beginning to think Frank was right, though. The only real proof she had of the mark was a questionable, grainy photo. Every other bit of information she had managed to gather all pointed in the same direction, that O'Donnell really did it. "Makes for a really short story," she told him.

Denny quickly pointed out, "You may be right, but doesn't it make you wonder why the Police aren't letting the press anywhere near O'Donnell? Not a single reporter has even been able to get close to him."

Vicky agreed, but then started to wonder who was the real reporter here. She was surprised that this thought hadn't occurred to her already. "You're right. You'd think a guy who'd killed the Mayor because he was trying to make a statement would want to talk to anybody he could."

Denny handed her another file folder. "I did some digging on Brent Gregor, too. I found out that he's spent thousands of dollars trying to walk again. He's traveled all over the world, tried every cure in the book. It's his obsession."

Vicky looked at the information curiously. This would have really been very handy *before* she had attempted to meet with him. Vicky perused the file. More than one clipping had a photo of Abigail Wentworth.

"What's it say about *her*?" Vicky asked. Vicky only knew the young Miss Wentworth from the few items she'd read about her aerial exploits, such as flying non-stop from New York to Mexico City and placing second in the Bendix race from Burbank to Cleveland.

"Just the usual batch of society articles from when they were an item," Denny replied. "Nothing about her flying accomplishments. That would be in another file."

"So, they're not together anymore?" Vicky asked.

"No," Denny offered, not exactly comfortable to talk about someone else's romantic life, particularly with Vicky. "Apparently they, uh... had some sort of falling out during a trip to India a few years ago."

Denny looked up to judge her reaction. Apparently, she thought of it just the same as any other bit of research, judging by her unchanged expression.

"That's not a hard one to figure out," Vicky offered, never taking her eyes off the articles in the folder. "She's free as a bird and he's stuck on the ground. Not to mention the fact that he's a complete crumb."

Vicky flipped back to the front of the folder. "You think there's anything to it?"

"To what?" Denny asked, puzzled. "The falling out in India?"

"No," Vicky corrected him with a quick sniff. She'd

completely changed gears and he hadn't been able to keep up. "His obsession. Trying to walk again."

"Not really," answered Denny. "Just an observation."

Vicky pondered Brent Gregor's situation, then asked, "Hey, if you had that kind of money, wouldn't you do the same?"

ANGELO TESTA sat down on a wooden crate outside of DeMarco's fish market with a fresh bucket of clams. His friend and fellow Soldato, Tommy Auferio looked at him with disgust.

"How can you eat those things raw?" Tommy asked with a pained expression.

"What? They're good!" Angelo proclaimed as he slurped up a gooey portion and let it slide down his throat.

"I can't watch this," Tommy said as he shook his head. "I'm gonna get a drink. You want anything?"

"No, I'm good," Angelo mumbled as he downed yet another.

"Yeah, you're good all right," Tommy replied as he got up and took a customary look around. It had been a quiet day in the South Side. He liked it that way.

Had Tommy waited just a moment longer, he would have noticed the dark green car that slowed down as it passed by the front of the market. Had Angelo not been so engrossed in his clams, he would have noticed it, too. Especially when the car pulled over across the street with the motor running.

Angelo had no inkling of the fair-haired man carrying a shotgun close to his side as he hurried across the street towards him. He never saw him or the riot gun until it was too late. He had reached into the bucket for yet another bite when the man stopped directly in front of him and raised his weapon. Angelo barely had time to register what was happening when the man pumped the weapon and pulled the trigger to produce a rapid volley of three shotgun blasts that knocked him backwards against the wall. The sound of the blasts echoed through the neighborhood. The bucket went flying with empty, blood-spattered clamshells scattered about the sidewalk.

The man wasted no time as he raced back to the waiting car. Tommy ran out of the market just as they sped off and disappeared around the next corner.

He rushed over to the screaming Angelo and the clamshells crunched against the bloody pavement under his feet. He had to look away. Angelo's face, neck, and shoulder had been chewed away by the shotgun blasts. His left arm had nearly been severed from his body. The pool of blood on the sidewalk grew like a rising tide.

Angelo cried out for his mother.

Tommy crossed himself and backed away into the swiftly gathering crowd of shocked and disgusted onlookers. It was luck that he was alive.

Pure luck indeed.

CHAPTER TEN

THAT night, Vicky drove over to Harvey O'Donnell's apartment building. She parked a good distance down the street, and sat in her car for a few minutes to study the building. She quickly realized that she should have thought this through a little more beforehand. She needed to get inside that apartment, though, and talk to Mrs. O'Donnell. Of course, her plan was to lie her way in. The best that she had been able to come up with was to pose as a church worker "concerned about the boys." As she reached for the door handle she realized that she looked nothing like a church worker. She looked exactly like what she was — a girl reporter. Again, her desire to grab the story had gotten the best of her. The least she could do is make an attempt, so she fastened the top button on her blouse.

Just as she was about to get out of her small coupe, the neighborhood patrol car pulled up behind her, driving slowly up the street. She quickly ducked down to let it pass, then hopped out and worked her way through the shadows towards the O'Donnell family's humble housing. It occurred to her that this was the part of reporting she seemed to be best at — the sneaking and snooping. She needed to work on the actual reasoning and deduction parts, what one does with the information gathered, if she were to continue surviving the sneaking and snooping. Sooner or later she was going to run out of luck, and information has always been the best weapon.

Vicky quietly climbed the building's staircase and found O'Donnell's apartment on the third floor. She started to knock, trying to remember a good Bible verse, and then noticed a window just past the landing. The blinds were partially open. If she could lean over just enough, she might be able to peer inside. It certainly beat the lame story she had concocted to worm her way inside.

She looked around at the nearby apartments. The last thing she needed right then was a nosy neighbor. There was one window directly across from her. The lights were on inside, but the blinds were closed. A bigger worry, she quickly realized, was the distance between the landing and the O'Donnell's window. Getting a better look, she realized that this would be harder than it had first appeared. Maybe she'd better go with the church worker story after all. No amount of supplication would save her if she toppled over the side. It was a straight drop all the way down.

Steeling what little courage she had at the moment, Vicky hopped onto the railing, sitting backwards, and prayed that it would hold. It was an old building, after all. She dropped her shoes on the wooden planking and gripped her feet around the rungs. She leaned back until she was able to grab the window sill for balance. Her heart skipped a beat or two until she was sure that her grip was firm enough and that the railing wouldn't collapse beneath her.

Fortunately, she was able to peer through the blinds and get a good look inside at Mrs. Ruth O'Donnell and her two young boys. That was when she saw something that rather surprised her: for a family that was destitute, supposedly so destitute that it inspired O'Donnell to write all those "threatening" letters to Mayor Nibley, they seemed to be getting on rather well. And now that Mr. O'Donnell was in prison, one would think that the family was even more destitute than before. Yet, there was food aplenty on the table, and the boys had several brand new toys scattered about the floor.

And what was more, Mrs. O'Donnell was wearing what looked to be a brand new pearl necklace. With earrings to match.

Vicky was now convinced. There was definitely something going on here. She hadn't quite uncovered it yet, but this gave her the impetus to dig deeper.

She shifted forward just enough to regain her forward balance and sat back up. She was quite relieved to hop back off the railing, back to the safety of the solid landing beneath her. She landed, however, with a much louder thud than she had intended. She stood perfectly still for a moment, not even taking a breath. She looked up at the neighbor's window. Fortunately, there was no sign of movement. Then she remembered the O'Donnell's window behind her and the fact that she was standing right in front of their door. If that door were to fling open, she'd need to come up with something fast. Perhaps she'd have to use the missionary story after all. Cautiously, she peered back over her shoulder. Thankfully, there were no faces at the window. And the door remained shut.

She breathed a quick sigh of relief, scooped up her shoes and on silent bare feet, headed back down the steps. She waited until she had gotten all the way to the grass before putting her heels back on, and even then thought twice about whether or not she should.

As Vicky scurried back to her coupe, hoping to get there before the neighborhood patrol car reappeared, she failed to notice the dark blue, four-door sedan that was parked further down the street. Had she seen it, she might have also noticed the man inside. He watched her every move as she got back into her vehicle and drove away. The car followed right behind and she paid it no mind. It wasn't until several blocks later, after it had continued behind her for two turns, when she began to suspect that she was being followed.

It could have been a coincidence, but she wanted to be sure. She turned right at the next corner and the car turned right. She nervously kept her eyes focused on the rear view mirror, watching the two ominous headlights behind her, and almost ran into a parked truck.

She went two more blocks and turned left. The car turned left. At the next intersection, she turned right again and kept on turning right at every until she had gone in a complete circle, back in the direction she had been going to start with.

The car was still behind her.

NO DOUBT about it. Vicky was definitely being followed. Perhaps it was only to intimidate her, and if that were the case, it was certainly working. But she couldn't be sure that intimidation was the driver's only plan.

Not wanting to panic, she breathed in deeply and tried to think of what to do. Stay on the main roads, for one. And don't stop for anything, not even a traffic light if she could help it. Just then she had a close call, almost getting snagged by a red light, but she managed to cruise through the intersection. The car following her slowed down then ran the traffic light to keep up.

Her heart raced and she had to remind herself over and over to stay calm. Just as she'd told herself earlier at Mrs. O'Donnell's apartment, she had to think and learn to reason if she were to survive the snooping. She just didn't think it would happen so soon.

Luckily, there was a Police Station not too far away. She'd have to cut down a narrow side street, but it would be the safest place to go. She definitely didn't want to go home. Not yet.

She decided to wait until the last second to turn. She was almost through the intersection when she whipped the steering wheel sharply to the left, then jammed the gas pedal to the floor. The car behind her had to make a sudden stop to follow.

Taking a quick look back, she thought that this maneuver had bought her another minute, perhaps enough of a safety net to make it to the next major road? As her heart continued to beat through her chest, she could only hope. Giving in to panic, she sped to the next intersection and quickly took a right before the car managed to catch up.

The police station was just a few blocks away. She felt herself calm some more as she hit the final stretch. She didn't mind gaining some attention for herself, even if it meant getting a ticket. That would have been the least of her worries.

She zipped through the last two blocks and practically slid to a stop in front of the Police Station. There were two uniformed Officers standing outside. They took quite a notice of her driving.

The car cruised casually by as one Officer strolled up to her window. "Everything all right, ma'am?"

"Officer," she told him, breathless. "That car was following me." She pointed him towards the passing vehicle.

The Officer looked up just in time to see the car's tail lights as it rounded the next corner. "Are you sure? Did you get a good look at it?" he asked.

"Yes, I'm sure. But I'm afraid I didn't see much more than the headlights. It was dark in color. Green maybe. I think they were after me. I'm a reporter, for the *Crusader*. Vicky Rose."

"Well, Miss Rose," he answered. "If you want to come in and file a report, we'll put out a bulletin for all the units in the area. Then we can have one of the men take you home."

"Thank you, Officer," she replied. "That would be very nice."

Frank had been right. These were people that were not to be dealt with lightly. She would have to be more careful from now on. As much as the event unnerved her, though, it hadn't been enough to shake her resolve. Still, as much as she wanted to stop at the Carousel, she went straight home and locked the doors securely. Sleeping was a nearly fruitless venture.

VICKY wasn't the only one who couldn't sleep that night. In Lakeview Heights, Brent Gregor lay in his grand master bed and stared out the window at the far off moon. His thoughts were in another part of the world, only he didn't know where. All he could think about was Abbie and the last time they'd seen each other. And how terribly it had gone wrong.

Their introduction hadn't begun much better.

CHAPTER ELEVEN

ABIGAIL WENTWORTH, and her old brother Billy, had lived in the mansion estate next door. From his bedroom window, in what used to be his parents' room, Brent could barely see the rooftop of their house in the distance, just behind the trees. He'd known Abbie since they were small children. She'd been there that fateful Halloween night and was brave enough herself to go up to the door of the Patterson House and look inside.

When Brent came home from the hospital several weeks later, from that point on confined to a wheelchair and likewise his own home, he was no longer able to play with the other boys in the neighborhood. Nanny Miriam, a short, portly woman with a round cheerful face, draped in an ever-present white smock (Brent never once saw her out of it), thought that was possibly a blessing in disguise since young Brent was then free of the corrupting influence of Julius Kennelly.

Still, the boy needed the companionship of children his own age. There were a few vain attempts to get Billy and some of the other neighborhood boys to come over periodically, but they were restless and filled with energy, and keeping them inside with young Brent was always a failed exercise. After Billy was sent home early one day, his mother, Mrs. Wentworth, a refined and soft-spoken woman, brightened upon an idea she thought was quite good. Little Abigail was too young to play with the other children, and her mother felt it was unladylike for Abbie to play outside anyway. So, she conspired with Nanny Miriam for Abbie to become Brent's regular playmate.

This was the worst thing that could have happened to him. He still remembered, as if it had happened the day before, the day she came over for the first time. Nanny Miriam was beside herself with anticipation and paced the foyer anxiously, waving her hands up by her round face. Agnes, the head housekeeper and Nanny Miriam's closest friend on staff (mostly because she was closest in age), stood sentry by Brent's wheelchair, ready to cart him up to the front door "just as soon as the glorious moment arrived."

Worthington had voiced his objections to the whole affair and had wisely made himself scarce. Brent wished that he could have done the same.

Finally, the doorbell rang and Nanny Miriam sprang like a ballerina to open the front door. She screamed with delight, which must have scared poor Mrs. Worthington to death, judging by the frightened look on her face when she entered. She greeted Nanny Miriam with an amazing display of restrained tolerance then beckoned young Abigail to follow her inside.

In came little Abigail in a neatly pressed pink dress and white stockings, with her light brown hair in two perfectly even pigtails tied in pink ribbons on each side. She even had pink ribbons on the tops of her shiny white shoes.

She entered like a delicate flower and stood silently until her mother softly whispered Nanny Miriam's name as a gentle reminder. Then Abigail performed a light curtsy and said in her small voice, "Good afternoon, Nanny Miriam. It's a pleasure to see you to-day."

Nanny Miriam let out another ear-shattering squeal of delight, which was clearly Agnes' cue to wheel young Brent across the bumpy carpet and up towards the waiting guests.

"Oh, it's so good to see you, too, Little Abigail. So sweet! Such a pretty dress, too!" Nanny Miriam chirped.

"Thank you, Nanny Miriam," Abigail offered again, at which Nanny Miriam let out another squeal, though this time much more contained.

It was at that moment that all of them turned their

heads, huge smiles plastered on their faces, as if they had been perfectly synchronized, directly towards Brent. He just sat there and stared back at them. Clearly they expected something, but he had no idea what.

Finally, Nanny Miriam broke the silence through still-smiling and un-moving teeth. "Brent? Don't you have something to say to little Abigail?"

"Oh," he replied as it finally dawned on him, struggling to remember the short speech he'd been instructed to recite. "It's, uh, lovely... to have you here to-day, too." He let out a quick sigh of relief at getting the words out, secretly wishing that with the pleasantries finally over, that she would just go home. No such luck.

With a few more barely suppressed squeals, Nanny Miriam secured the details of Abigail's stay and eventual return before ushering Mrs. Wentworth out. Agnes asked Abigail to follow her as she quickly wheeled Brent into the former music room that (aside from the grand piano that still resided in there) had been converted into Brent's first-floor playroom, where all of his toys and books were kept. Even though the house was equipped with an elevator, it was much easier to confine him to the ground floor for the entire day before retiring upstairs at night.

Nanny Miriam arrived only seconds behind them and immediately gave deference to Abigail's wishes as she organized their activities for the afternoon.

"So, Abigail, she asked, "what would *you* like to do today?"

"I would like to have a tea party, thank you," Abigail said oh-so politely that Nanny Miriam barely suppressed another squeal.

"Why, yes, of course, Dear!" Nanny Miriam answered, then quickly ordered Agnes to rush off to the kitchen and have Chef Jerome to prepare a small teapot with milk and cookies.

Brent thought his disagreement in the choice of activity had fallen on deaf ears until he repeated it a second time, much louder. "But I don't want to have a tea party."

"Now Brent," Nanny Miriam answered, ever smiling, "Abigail is our guest and we need to make her feel welcome."

Brent wasn't sure, but he thought he sensed a bit of

self-satisfaction from Abigail for getting her way as she sat
daintily at his table.

"Now, Brent" (he would here his name spoken this way
often) orchestrated Nanny Miriam as she ushered Abigail
over to his small table that he had covered with the pieces
to a half-completed puzzle, "let's put this puzzle away so
that we can have somewhere to sit. I've told you before not
to leave your toys out."

"But I'm still working on it," Brent protested to no avail.
Instead, Nanny Miriam grabbed the box and raked the
entirety of it back in and quickly dispensed it on the shelf.
All that work gone to waste, Brent grumbled to himself.
He'd been laboring at that puzzle for days and had been
finally making progress.

Just when Brent didn't think it could get any worse,
Nanny Miriam grabbed the handles of his wheelchair and
unceremoniously shoved him to up to the table. How he
wished he'd had a hand brake so that he could have at
least slowed her down a bit. But no, he immediately found
himself seated across from Abigail's little smiling face. He
would much rather have been alone.

Moments later, Agnes returned with the tea tray and set
it down on the table between them. Brent just folded his
arms and glowered back.

"Why thank you, Mrs. Agnes," chirped Abigail cheerily.
"Brent, would you like to have some tea?" she asked.

Again, all eyes were on him. He looked first at Abigail,
then at Agnes (who wasn't really a Mrs.), and finally at
Nanny Miriam. They were all impatiently waiting.

"Yes, please," he mumbled reluctantly.

Oh, the indignity. Thank goodness neither Julius
Kennelly nor any of the other boys could see him. At least
some good came of the fact that they always played outside.
That was quite the consolation. But it only lasted for a brief
second. Surely, he realized, Abigail would tell her brother,
Billy, and then it would get out. And that would be the
ultimate humiliation.

It was.

Julius Kennelly already took every opportunity to tease
him for "being a cripple" and having a "mother in the

asylum." This was just more fuel for the fire. And what fuel it was at that.

On Abigail's second visit, Brent discovered that Abigail was a "tattle-tail." Even worse was that it worked. Abigail brought over several of her dolls and, after the tea party was over, wanted Brent to play.

Naturally, he protested in the strongest possible terms.

"I told you, I don't want to play with your stupid dolls!"

Brent thought she would burst into tears, but instead she shouted at the top of her lungs, with her eyes locked solidly on him in a look of vengeance as she screamed, "Nanny Miriam! Brent won't let me play with my dolls!"

Nanny Miriam immediately rushed to Abigail's side, kissed her on the forehead, and promptly chastised him. "Now, Brent!" she scolded. "Abigail is our guest!"

It would become a common refrain. She'd always wanted a daughter of her own and caring for little Abigail was the closest she would ever come.

"Nanny Miriam! Brent won't let me play with my dolls!"

"Nanny Miriam! Brent told me tea parties are stupid!"

"Nanny Miriam! Brent won't let me read his book!"

Play date after play date, Abigail would get him in trouble, sometimes when he had said nothing at all. And every time, Nanny Miriam would rush to Abigail's aid, offer loving consolation, and kiss her on the forehead. As soon as Nanny Miriam turned to Brent, Abigail would secretly stick her tongue out at him. That little girl was pure evil, but he was completely powerless to do anything about it.

Years later, Abbie would apologize to him profusely and more than make it up to him for her gross manipulation of Nanny Miriam. But poor Brent had no way of knowing at the time how differently things would one day transpire.

Eventually, much to Brent's relief, as the two of them hit their early teenage years, Mrs. Wentworth rethought the idea of them spending so much time together and brought their regular play dates to a sudden end. Even though she lived next door, the Wentworth Mansion was still far enough away that he rarely saw Abigail after that and then just from a distance. On the few occasions that he did, he could only tell that she had grown taller. But to him, she would always be the same irritating girl with whom he'd been forced to play "girl games."

Then she was sent away to a preparatory school for girls and that was the last he saw of her for ages. Good riddance, he thought.

ONE could only imagine his great surprise when, years later, he finally ran into her again on campus at college. Determined to gain a measure of independence, Brent had moved to the campus at Emerson University, an old university that originated in the early-1800s with historic, Colonial-style firebrick buildings and brick sidewalks that must have taken several brigades of artisans a decade or more to lay. For the first time in his life, he left Worthington, Nanny Miriam, and the other servants back at the mansion. His first attempt at self-sufficiency didn't go as well as planned (he was too used to having a cadre of servants at his beck and call), so he was forced to hire a student to sometimes help with his chair and books.

During his second year, his student aide was a young blonde-haired fellow named Stephen Praisner, who was there on a full scholarship for the men's swim team and loved to read pulp novels and other fantasy stories. The autumn leaves were just about to turn and Stephen was still getting the hang of navigating Brent's chair down the bumpy brick sidewalks.

One such morning, Brent looked ahead in his vain attempt to remain dignified when he was taken in by a true vision that approached before him. She was a beautiful young swan with long, flowing brunette locks that framed her lightly-freckled face and cascaded down her shoulders. Even in her plain school uniform of a white shirt, plaid skirt and dark blue stockings, her natural radiance and unadorned beauty out-shown everyone else around her. He was in awe.

Brent was stunned when the beautiful girl smiled back at him. He was even more stunned when his chair caught in the sidewalk and he was nearly thrown headlong onto the bricks. Like a guardian angel, she rushed to his aide and clutched his shoulders to keep him from falling.

"Are you all right?" she asked.

Her voice was soft and melodic. And oddly familiar.

"Yes, yes, thank you," he replied as he looked up. Her eyes were familiar, too.

Stephen was gravely apologetic. "Sorry, so sorry..."

"Brent?" the girl asked. That was when he recognized her, too.

"Abigail?" he asked in return, too dumbstruck to say anything more.

Her face lit up at the realization. "Oh, my heavens! I don't believe it. I haven't seen you in ages!"

Brent couldn't believe it, either. This was the girl with whom he'd been forced to play with dolls and have tea parties. How time had changed things. His childhood resentment, or a good enough portion of it at least, immediately vanished.

He finally collected himself enough to speak.

"How long have you been going here?" he asked.

"It's my first year. I just started," she answered and her smile grew brighter by the minute.

Stephen stood awkwardly behind Brent's chair. As much as he appreciated their joyful reunion (not to mention that she was quite lovely to look at), he had to get Brent to class so that he could then rush off to his own. At this point, they barely had enough time to make it.

"Uh, Mr. Gregor..." Stephen interrupted with hesitation.

Brent turned around then blushed.

"I'm sorry," Brent told her, "where are my manners? Abigail, this is Stephen. He helps me out. Stephen, this is my..." he stumbled for just the right words, then continued, "old friend. Abigail. We grew up next door to one another."

A look of puzzled sadness crossed her face. "Is Worthington...?"

"Oh, no, he's perfectly fine," Brent exclaimed as he realized her concern. "College just isn't the place for him, you know. Nanny Miriam, Agnes, Sally — they're all well."

Abigail was quite relieved to hear it.

Stephen attempted another sheepish interruption. "Uh, Mr. Gregor, we *really* need to get to class."

"Oh, right!" Brent exclaimed. He'd completely forgotten.

He looked back at Abigail and immediately realized that the thought of attending class meant nothing to him at that moment.

"I tell you what," he said to Stephen, "Why don't you just go on? I'll be fine."

"Really? Thank you, Sir!" Stephen exclaimed as he scooped up his textbooks and raced off.

Brent turned back and looked her over again. "I just can't get over how much you've changed."

"So have you," she said back with a smile.

"Well, I suppose I'm a bit taller," he replied. "But it's hard to tell because I'm always sitting down."

They had a good chuckle. Brent liked the sound of her unrestrained laughter. He could tell immediately that she was different from the other girls there — so free and informal. And so very much unlike her mother.

She really liked seeing him smile.

The clock tower chimed the afternoon hour. It was two o'clock. Abigail's expression grew a bit concerned.

"Oh, my, I'm afraid I'm late for class myself," she said, ready to rush off like Cinderella from the ball.

Brent quickly reached out for her hand.

"Do you really have to go?" he asked.

She thought nervously for a moment. Her mind told her one thing, but her heart clearly told her something else.

"No," she answered and her smile brightened again.

"What do you say we go get something and catch up?" he asked.

"Yes, I'd love to," she told him.

That was all he needed to hear. Brent grabbed the wheels of his chair and attempted to turn it back around. But it was still stuck in the rut of the sidewalk.

"Why don't you let me drive?" she asked, then grabbed the handles and tipped him lightly backwards. She wheeled him back around and pushed him gently off. "I always wanted to push you around. I used to love it when Nanny Miriam would shove you under that table."

"Yes, I know," Brent replied, shaking his head at the memory. But he could hardly believe that this was the same girl that had so tortured him for those many years.

WITHIN minutes they had reached Cameron Street, the main thoroughfare on the edge of campus that was littered with pubs, cafés, and shops of every kind. Abbie immediately steered him into the first establishment she found — Edgar's, a quaint little dive that was part café, part bookstore and inspired by the works of Poe. There was a large, photographic portrait of the author on one wall, a stuffed raven with glowing red eyes perched atop the foremost bookshelf, and a large cutout of the word "Nevermore!" hanging from the ceiling. It certainly wasn't the most romantic of establishments, but neither of them cared.

"Can I get you something to eat? Something to drink?" Abbie offered.

"Tea, maybe?" Brent asked.

Abbie was halfway to the counter before she got the joke. She was tempted to order it anyway, but instead returned with a couple of fountain sodas.

The world around him seemed to completely slow down as she gently slid into the seat across from him. He still couldn't believe that evil little Abbie, who had *so* tortured him, would grow up to be this beautiful.

"So," she asked with a warm smile that just completely lit up the room, "how long have you been here?"

"Second year," Brent told her.

"Wow, really?" she responded with surprise. "I thought you were two years older than me at least."

"Oh, right," Brent answered, feeling slightly embarrassed. If it had been anyone else, he probably wouldn't have admitted the truth. "Worthington wasn't really in favor of me going off to school on my own, so he held me back a year until I finally convinced him. I think Nanny Miriam even did a lot of campaigning to convince him, too. I was just so glad to get out of that old house for change."

"Oh, I don't doubt it," she replied sympathetically, moving closer to him. I knew he was always protective, but really."

Just then her eyes lit up and she moved closer still.

"Did I ever tell you about the time he chastised me?" she asked, bursting at the seams to recount the tale.

"No," Brent replied, dying to hear every detail.

"First off," she began, "let me say that I am just so, *so* sorry for the way I tortured you. Believe me, it just kills me now when I think about it. You poor dear, how you survived it all those years, I have no idea. I am just — well, I can't apologize enough. And especially the way I manipulated poor Nanny Miriam. I just need to call her up one day and apologize, too."

Abbie stopped for a moment and pondered the thought. As much as Brent appreciated finally getting an apology, he was doubly anxious to hear the details of her story.

"Well, maybe not," she continued. "She should have known what I was up to. Heavens, it was just *so* obvious. But Worthington, he saw me one day. He *knew* what was going on. Then when it was time to leave that day, he offered to show me to the door."

"Yes," Brent said, "I think I remember that." It was such an unusual occasion for Worthington to even be seen during Abbie's visits, Brent had been even more surprised when he had reappeared and offered to escort her out.

"Well, we get out into the hallway, out of earshot from everyone, and he kneeled down right in front of me and got really close with that big, bushy beard, and said in that lovely British voice, 'Mistress Abigail.' I loved it when he called me 'Mistress Abigail,' but this time I could tell he really meant business."

Abbie did her best to interpret Worthington's melodious voice, accent and all. "'Mistress Abigail, I think it would behoove you to treat Master Gregor with the epitome of kindness and respect.' Then he just stared at me with that stern expression he used (Brent knew it well) for a moment before he stood up and walked me the rest of the way. That was all he said. I had no idea what 'behoove' or 'epitome' meant, but I knew *exactly* what he did."

Brent looked back at her, puzzled. "I don't remember you treating me any nicer."

"Of course, not," she smiled. "I just made extra sure Worthington wasn't around when I didn't."

With that, she leaned forward and gave him a quick kiss on the cheek.

"Forgive me?" she asked, smiling.

He didn't know whether he was being manipulated again or not, but he clearly had no choice.

"Of course," he answered back.

She flopped back in her chair, her eyes never leaving him, even as a lock of her beautiful hair fell down in front of her face. "I always hated our get-togethers," she confessed. "I so much wanted to go outside with Billy and just run my heart out. But mother wouldn't allow it. It was all I could do to escape from time to time."

He loved the way the light caught her eyes when she smiled. He just couldn't believe that this was the same girl he'd dreaded so much before.

THEY had no idea how long they'd even been there until the sun went down outside and the café was ready to close. They were both stunned to find out just how late it was.

"Oh heavens, Mrs. Fruehauf is going to think I died," Abbie exclaimed. "Probably already called my mother."

"Can I take you home?" Brent asked.

"Too bad we don't live next door anymore," she replied. "Well, not here anyway."

As Brent struggled to maneuver his chair out of the café, Abbie could sense the Owner's growing impatience.

"Here, let me help," she volunteered, and quickly commandeered the handles, spun him around the tables and towards the front door. The Owner had to quicken his pace to catch up with her and hold the door open. Brent was bumped up out of his seat and had to hang on as Abbie barreled him over the threshold. The Owner locked the door behind them as she hurriedly pushed him down the sidewalk back towards campus and the girl's dormitory.

"I think this is more like me taking *you* home," she remarked with a grin.

It turned out that their dorms weren't that far apart at all. Perhaps nearly as close as their homes in Lakeview Heights.

"I hate coming back here at night," she confessed. Brent could immediately see why.

"Looks a lot like the old Patterson house," he replied.

"Remember how Julius used to make us go up on the

porch every year and look inside?" she asked, then added without thinking. "You only had to do that once." Then she suddenly remembered the reason why and quickly apologized.

"It's okay," Brent told her. Despite the fact that it was still a rather sore subject, it wasn't like he wasn't reminded of it every day.

"I have another confession to make," Abbie told him as she pushed his chair up to the steps and sat across from him, completely forgetting that she had been in a hurry. "That first time I went up there, I had my eyes closed the whole time. Julius didn't notice because he was paying too much attention to you. Shut my eyes every time after that, too."

Brent smiled at hearing the truth, and also because it turned out that he had been braver than her after all.

"So," she asked, "you see Julius anymore?"

Brent shook his head in disgust. "I'd be more than happy to never see him again. He's at Harvard. Hope he stays there."

"See," she told him, "there *is* someone you disliked more than me. Of course, he does set the bar rather low."

They sat there quietly for just a moment until their mutual distaste dissolved into laughter. Brent was glad that she felt the same way he did.

"He tried to kiss me once," she blurted out. She was full of confessions that night. Brent's ears perked up. "In high school. I think he did it on a dare. Either way, he thought I would swoon over him like every other girl."

She let the thought hang in the air just to see how long it took him to respond. She didn't have to wait.

"What happened?" he asked, anxiously.

"I kicked him in the shin," she chuckled with pride. "I would have kicked him somewhere else, too, but Mrs. Gartner caught me and drug us both off to the office."

"You didn't get in trouble, did you?" Brent asked.

"No, I just had to cry for a bit. I could work her just like Nanny Miriam. Julius got the paddle. He deserved it," she answered with an air of satisfaction.

Brent had to admit that he was glad to hear Julius had at

least experienced some modicum of justice in his life. And that she had actually given Julius worse than she had ever given him.

As he looked into her eyes and saw the moonlight reflected from above, he wanted nothing more than to stand up from his chair and kiss her himself. From that moment on he was certain that they were destined to be together.

Just then, Mrs. Fruehauf (Abbie had serious doubts that she'd ever actually been married), the large, stern Girls' Dorm Matron, marched out and ordered Abbie inside, holding the door open for her.

"Yes, Ma'm," Abbie replied obediently as she hopped quickly to her feet. Clearly, her powers of manipulation hadn't worked with this woman.

Abbie stopped for a moment when she reached the door, and asked, "You sure you can get back on your own?"

"Of course," he assured her. "The sidewalks are much smoother here. I'll be fine."

She offered a quick "See you tomorrow" then blew him a kiss and disappeared. He would have to wait a bit longer for a real one.

Mrs. Fruehauf glared sternly at Brent until he turned his chair around and was well on his way down the sidewalk. Confined to a wheelchair or not, he was still a member of the male species and, therefore, not to be trusted in any capacity.

It mattered little whether the sidewalks were bumpy or not. Brent practically floated back to his dorm that night.

He and Abbie were nearly inseparable for the longest time after that day except for one thing that never failed to come between them — Brent's inability to walk. Abbie was a free spirit who longed to do things and go places that Brent just couldn't do. He always felt like he was the anchor that held her down, the chains that bound her angelic wings to the Earth. Abbie needed to fly, literally, and she burned to see the world.

Brent knew that if he could ever walk again, that if he could be cured and become the man that she needed, that he and Abbie could finally be together.

That is, if she were to ever take him back.

As the morning sun broke through the window, Brent was ready to try again to walk. And if he were finally successful, he was ready to find her.

CHAPTER TWELVE

THE impatient crowd backed away from the tracks as the thundering locomotive pulled into the Terminal City Depot. The train was over twenty minutes late. Almost before it came to a complete stop, the passengers began to disembark, ready to meet with their waiting friends and family members, or move on to their next destinations. Porters rushed around with carts to assist with luggage. There was no shortage of people who needed their services.

One of the last to step from the train, carrying only a single suitcase and a weathered, ornately-designed red box fastened tightly with a thin leather strand wrapped many times around, was an old Gypsy Woman in a long, brightly-patterned dress and draped with multiple scarves. The lines on her face spoke of years of experience and wisdom.

No one paid her any mind as she shuffled through the crowd. None but a tall, distinguished English gentleman, who stood straight and firm beside a waiting car. As soon as he spotted her in the crowd, he knew he had found the right person. She'd sent word that he'd know her by sight, and she'd been correct.

"Madame Ouspenskaya, I presume?" Worthington asked, stumbling, slightly, over the unfamiliarity of the name.

"Yes, it is I," the old woman answered, giving as much of a curtsy as her old bones would allow.

"The car is waiting right over here, Madame. Master Gregor is most anxious to see you right away," Worthington said as he led her to the long, black automobile. "Do you have any other luggage, Madame?"

"No," she told him. "Only this."

Worthington opened the car door and took the suitcase, but she refused to give up the box. "I must carry this myself," she told him firmly.

"Very well, Madame," answered Worthington, closing the car door and putting the suitcase in the trunk. If she'd never been in such a fine car before, she gave no evidence of it. She just sat quietly in the back as Worthington climbed in and drove her straight to the Gregor Mansion, just has he'd been instructed.

AS SOON as they arrived at the great house, Worthington carried her suitcase and led her, still clutching the box, upstairs and down the long hallway. They stopped briefly at one of the grandly furnished guest rooms to drop off her luggage.

"I think you'll be very comfortable in here, Madame," Worthington told her. She only nodded and briefly looked around, but again gave no recognition to the opulence that surrounded her.

"I'll be glad to unpack your things and show you around later," Worthington offered, "but I'm afraid Master Gregor wishes to see you straight away. I'm surprised that he hasn't rung for you already. This way, please."

She only nodded again and followed him back out, box in hand, and down the lengthy hallway. They finally came to a stop outside the Master Bedroom, all the way at the very end.

Worthington asked, "If you don't mind, Madame, could you please wait here for just a moment?"

She gave a short nod and Worthington slipped into Brent Gregor's quarters, quietly closing the door behind him.

Brent Gregor maintained his usual post, sitting in his wheelchair, staring at the world outside his window. "Is she here?" he asked.

"Yes, Sir," Worthington answered.

"Then why haven't you brought her in?" Brent demanded. "I told you to bring her straight to me."

"Yes, Sir," Worthington replied. "I just wished to

respectfully implore once more, Sir. This woman is a fraud, I am sure of it. I strongly suggest that you turn her away at once."

Brent glared at Worthington. "Send her in and leave us."

"Yes, Sir," Worthington complied, his head low. He showed Madame Ouspenskaya into the room and closed the door as he left. Worried for Brent's safety, he stood outside the room and clutched the many-beaded rosary in his pocket while he listened and waited.

"Madame Ouspenskaya," Brent said to her. "I can't thank you enough for traveling all this way. I am truly honored. You can help me?"

"Yes," she answered.

"What must I do?" he pleaded.

She placed the box on the small table, stepped closer to him and took his hand. She studied it carefully, traced the lines on his palm, then looked deep into his eyes.

"There is a Spirit Force," she began. "By harnessing its healing power, you can be made whole and to walk again."

Brent smiled in desperation. For these last fifteen difficult years, these were the words he most longed to hear. Despite how incredible they may have seemed to any other ears.

Madame Ouspenskaya continued, "Joining with the Spirit Force will give you not just the ability to walk, but great power. Yet it comes with a price."

Brent pleaded, "What price? I'll pay anything."

She gripped his hand tightly. "It is not a price that you can pay with currency. Your riches are worthless as far as the Spirit Force is concerned. It is a price that you must pay with your heart. And with your soul."

Worthington listened intently from outside the door. This was exactly as he had feared. Whether she were a fraud or performing the will of the Devil himself, no good could ever come of what she had to offer, of that he was sure.

"You must use this power to bring justice to those who have none," she told Brent. "If you do not, then the Spirit Force will leave you and you will never be able to use its power again."

Brent agreed. "Yes! Whatever the cost! I'll gladly do it!"

She released his hand and backed away. "The last one to join with the Spirit Force was blind, and it allowed him to see. Its effects are different for each person that joins with it. If the ailment is great, such as yours, it will not be as strong as it would be for one who is whole. It will give you strength and agility, the ability to walk. But it will also give you spectral abilities. To hide in the shadows and pass by others unseen. Locked doors will no longer contain you. You may also command objects to move without touching them."

Madame Ouspenskaya reached in her dress pocket and produced a gold ring with a fire-red opal. "This ring," she told him, "carries the Spirit Force within. When you put it on your finger, you and the Spirit Force will be joined together. Even if you take off the ring, the Spirit Force will still be with you. Do you accept this great responsibility?"

"Yes!" Brent shouted, almost maniacally.

Worthington could take no more. He burst into the room, flinging the doors wide, challenging Madame Ouspenskaya like a Priest confronting Satan. "Sir! I beg you! Her rantings are the work of the Devil! Dispose of her, please!"

Madame Ouspenskaya stepped back and bowed her head quietly. Brent glowered at Worthington from his wheelchair. "Worthington, for as long as I have lived, you have been my most faithful and trusted servant. But on this occasion, I must ask you to leave and not interfere."

Worthington hung his head low. "If that is your wish then."

He left straight away. This time, he did not wait outside the room, but went to his quarters to pack his things. As much as he loved Master Gregor, he could not be a party to whatever dark magic this woman claimed to possess.

Madame Ouspenskaya directed Brent to the box on the table. "This box, do not open it until you are ready to seek justice. You will know when the time has come. Are you ready to be joined?" she asked, presenting the ring.

Brent hesitated for just a moment then took the ring from her. He studied it carefully for a long while. It had a dull gold band, decorated with intricate patterns that were black in their many crevices. In the center was a black opal that bore just a tint of red in the light.

He placed it on his finger. As soon as the ring reached the end of its path, a jolt of electricity surged through his body, causing him to shake and to scream out uncontrollably.

His screams reached Worthington's room at the end of the hall where he knelt in prayer, his rosary firmly in hand.

Just as he had feared. No good would come of this.

He was certain of it.

AS BRENT lay in his bed that night, after many hours of vain attempts to sleep, he awoke to absolute blackness, darker than pitch. He strained to see any sign of light, but there was none. Not in any direction.

"Worthington!" he cried out. There was no answer.

He shouted again. He felt a soft hand on his shoulder and a small, girlish voice whisper sharply in his ear. "Quiet! They're coming!"

Brent turned in the direction of the young girl's voice, but could see nothing. Then he felt her tug his arm quickly, and he fell to the rough-hewn floor. This wasn't his bedchamber.

She tugged at him again. "Come on!"

Instinctively, he followed. And to his great surprise, his legs moved with him. There was no dullness. No pain. It was as if he had never been lame.

He heard the sound of old hinges creak in the floor. She pulled him across the hard surface and his foot landed on empty space. "Careful," she said, panic in her voice.

She took his foot and guided it to a wooden step. He moved his hands closer and found that he was on a ladder. Sensing her fear and urgency, he climbed down quickly. She came right after him. Then he heard the trap door shut over their heads.

"Quiet!" she reminded him. "Or they'll hear us."

In the few moments of silence that remained, Brent was struck by the realization that he had been there before. He remembered this place. He knew the earthen floor beneath him, the musty smells all around, and the sound of her breathing.

Most of all, he realized that he wasn't surrounded by the darkness of night.

He was blind.

And these weren't his memories.

In the next second, he was jolted by a loud crashing sound in the hut above them. The door had been burst open, and was nearly knocked from its hinges. That was quickly followed by the sound of many boots stomping hurriedly on the floorboards above their heads.

Without realizing it, he counted three men.

He could sense the young girl's fear.

The trap door above their heads was quickly ripped open. She screamed and grabbed him tightly. He wanted to run, to protect her, but had no idea where to go.

He was helpless.

It was a feeling he knew from more than one lifetime.

Large, invading hands reached down into the pit. She screamed again and clutched him tightly.

He wanted to strike back.

But it was no use.

She cried out. "Let go!" They grabbed her and pulled her up. She screamed and fought, but was pulled from his grasp. As soon as she slipped away, four vice-like hands gripped around his arms and yanked him up as well. They threw him down to the floor.

He felt the rough surface again. He heard the crackling embers of the fire to his right. He knew exactly where he was.

He listened. He heard her cries and their laughter. One stood directly in front of him, just two paces away. The other two stood to his left, holding her as she struggled to free herself from their grasps. The first was looking in their direction.

He reached to his side. There, right where he remembered it was the fire poker. Slowly he reached out and wrapped his fingers around the iron handle.

He quickly lunged and in one hurried move, brought the poker down on the one in front of him. For once, the scream wasn't hers. He heard the man's body hit the floor.

"Run!" he shouted as one let go of her and came at him. He swung the poker again, but only found dead air before a sharp blow sent him unconscious to the floor.

THE NEXT morning, as Worthington gathered the last of his belongings, he watched from the window as Madame Ouspenskaya left the mansion. She boarded the taxi he had called and drove out of sight. He felt relief that she was gone, but troubled by what she had left in her wake.

Worthington carried his bags down to the foyer and deposited them there. He looked around the grand entryway, taking it in one last time. He has spent most of his life in this house. He had many fond memories there. He could still see Master Gregor as a child, running the hallways, his proud parents still young and beautiful. But those days were long gone, and he had no idea what the future had in store. He had only tried to leave once before, but fate had stepped squarely in his path and kept him from doing so.

This was the hardest thing he had ever done. The only thing left to do now was to deliver some papers to Master Gregor and inform him that he was leaving.

Worthington went up to Master Gregor's room where he found him, as expected, staring out the window from his wheelchair. Brent must have heard him enter, but didn't turn around to look.

Worthington cleared his throat quietly and said, "I'm leaving now, Sir. I just needed to give you these before I depart."

Brent turned to him with a look of fierce determination, his eyes dark from lack of sleep. "Before you go, I just want to show you one thing." Brent wheeled his chair around to face Worthington. He set his feet on the floor.

Worthington uttered a quick plea. "Master, please."

Slowly, Brent gripped the handles of the chair and lifted himself to a standing position. Worthington dropped his papers, completely taken aback. He crossed himself. "Oh, my! This is the work of the Devil!"

Brent smiled at him and said, "No, Worthington. How can you not recognize a miracle when you see it? Surely, this is the power of God!"

BRENT had Worthington drive him to the Cathedral of the Holy Name, where Worthington attended Mass every week (and often more than once). Brent had long since resigned from regular church visits (much to Worthington's consternation), but given the miracle they'd both witnessed, he felt a newfound urge to ponder his wondrous blessing in a more appropriate location.

After pulling their long, black limousine up to the curb of the church (the outside corner of which, oddly enough, still bore the bullet indentations from the ambush of North Side gang member Earl Murray), Worthington found Father Sean Ryan, a kind, stalwart man who'd served as a Chaplain during the Great War, waiting outside for them as requested. Worthington and Father Ryan helped Brent from the car and up the few stairs into the sanctuary (the difficulty involved with going was another reason Brent had given it up). Brent wished with all of his heart that he could have climbed the stairs himself, but having barely achieved the ability to stand, he was still a long way yet from that accomplishment.

Once they had gotten him settled back into his chair, Father Ryan offered Brent a hearty handshake and asked if he was there for confession.

"No," Brent replied, "I'd just prefer to go in and sit for a while."

"Of course," answered Father Ryan. "Take as much time as you need."

Worthington wheeled Brent down the center aisle and helped him into a pew some ten rows from the altar. After moving his wheelchair to the side, Worthington said, "If you don't mind, Sir, I rather feel the need to go to confession myself."

"Of course," Brent replied. "I'll be fine."

Worthington walked quietly off and left Brent alone with his thoughts.

As he stared up at the stained glass windows and large crucifix that hung above the altar, Brent could only ponder the steps that had led him there that peaceful night. He'd never been one to believe in miracles before — certainly not after the pain he'd experienced the last fifteen years. The loss of his parents and his ability to walk had certainly shaped his way of thinking since then. He hadn't given up on God, but he hadn't put his faith in Him, either. Despite being in his mid-20s, the seeds had already been sown for him to eventually become a bitter, lonely man. He never had any real friends growing up — only Worthington and the other servants who cared for him.

The one true bright spot in his life up until then had been Abbie. He couldn't help but smile every time he thought of her. Even in spite of what had happened in India. His entire outlook had changed when Abbie came back into his life.

She had changed everything.

Having her by his side opened new doors for him, both literally and figuratively. People who'd previously been anxious about speaking to "the stern-looking young man in the wheelchair" were more than willing to offer a friendly greeting to Abbie (and who wouldn't be?) and then to him as well. He was finally able to open up and experience life more fully.

And he owed it all to her.

He prayed that it could be that way again.

CHAPTER THIRTEEN

BRENT and Abbie had become nearly inseparable after their "re-acquaintance" at Emerson. So much so that it soon became a bit of a problem for Stephen, his student assistant. Brent was completely unaware of this fact (and to his credit, Abbie as well) until Stephen met them both in the cafeteria one day during lunch at one of the many small, square tables.

"Stephen! How are you?" Brent greeted him warmly. Quite the change from just a few weeks earlier. "Haven't seen you in days. Please, sit down."

"Thank you, Mr. Gregor," Stephen replied anxiously as he took a chair across from them. "Actually, that's kind of what I wanted to talk to you about."

Abbie let out a small girlish chuckle. Stephen looked to see if there was something wrong on his person.

"No, you're fine, Stephen," she replied. "You don't have to call him 'Mr. Gregor.' He's just 'Brent.'" She turned back to Brent with an accusatory smile. "Have you been making him call you that?"

Stephen looked back to Brent for approval. He smiled back in agreement, with his gaze firmly on her. "She's right, Stephen. My apologies. I grew up in a house full of servants. No offense to you, of course. It's just what I've been used to. Please, by all means, call me 'Brent' from now on. I promise, I won't answer to anything differently."

"So, what are you reading?" Abbie asked Stephen, noting the careworn, hardcover book he'd checked out of the campus library.

"Oh, this?" Stephen replied. "It's, uh... it's called *Esmerelda's Forest*. A bit of, uh... European fantasy literature from the early 1900s." Stephen tried to make it sound more "highbrow" than it actually was, and was secretly glad that she hadn't caught him reading Burroughs' *A Princess of Mars*, which he'd only just finished reading the week before. Stephen had quite a taste for "pulp" literature, though it didn't gain much respect in the halls of academia where he resided.

"Yes, I read that," Abbie answered excitedly. "It's really good. What part are you on?"

Brent just sat back and listened to their conversation and marveled at how well Abbie was able to connect with almost anyone she met.

"Oh, I just started it, really," Stephen perked up. "I've only gotten to the part where Esmerelda sees the shaft of light for the first time. I have to admit, the prose is almost lyrical."

Brent suspected that Stephen was no longer trying to sound "highbrow" on that last point. He really loved the book. Brent had never seen him so animated.

"Definitely," Abbie agreed. "We'll have to talk when you finish it. I'd *love* to get your take on the ending."

"Sure, sure," Stephen replied, excited to have found a kindred spirit but wanting to steer the conversation back to his issue with Brent. "I'd love to."

Brent could sense this as well. "So, Stephen, what was it you wanted to talk to me about?"

"Well, you see, it's about our... arrangement," Stephen replied, the anxiety returning to his voice. "You see, ever since you two... you know, well, I haven't really done *anything*. And I just don't feel it's right to, you know... keep taking the money."

"But you need it, don't you?" Brent asked. Abbie shot him a quick look to say that he was perhaps too blunt.

"Uh..." Stephen stammered, not sure how to respond. Yes, he desperately needed the money, but it wasn't something to which he readily wanted to admit. "It just doesn't seem right."

It was time for Abbie's diplomacy once again.

"There's no need to feel ashamed, Stephen," Abbie interjected as she reached out for his hand. "It's difficult for *everyone* these days. You've been a very good friend and Brent only wants to help. Besides, it would be *much* easier for him if you'd stay on at full salary." Abbie suspected she perhaps sounded too elite herself with that last bit of wording. "If he were to stop paying you, then Worthington would want to come out here and take charge of things, so really, you'd be doing Brent quite a favor."

Just a mention of Worthington's name immediately brought back memories of the thorough interview he'd undergone just to obtain his "position." He certainly didn't want to have to go through anything like that again — much less explain why he was abandoning it.

"Right," Stephen replied in full agreement. "That makes perfect sense." He sat there silently for another anxious moment then got up. "Well, if you'll excuse me, I have to get to class now. Umm, thank you. Very much."

"Thank you for stopping by, Stephen," replied Abbie cheerily. "It was great talking to you. I *can't wait* until you finish the book so we can talk some more."

She gave Brent a quick nudge under the table. "Yes," he added hastily. "We'll see you again soon."

As Stephen hurried off, Brent pondered in surprise, "Never knew he liked to read so much."

"That's because you never asked him," Abbie admonished playfully. "The rest of the world doesn't revolve around *you*, 'Mr. Gregor.' Only inside that big old house of yours."

It would not be the last time she told him that.

THE WEATHER began to turn cooler over the next two weeks and Brent quickly found that he had much less tolerance for the outdoors than Abbie. While she still favored evening strolls across the grounds, he was more than ready to call it a night as soon as the sun went down, despite how romantic the gas-lit campus was in the chill of the night air.

Finally, Abbie promised to spend their evenings indoors if he'd accompany her one last time out to the sports field to look at the stars. She loved little more than to stare up at the night sky. With her assurance that it would really be the last time until spring, Brent could only agree.

With the near-pitch darkness, getting there was much more difficult than either of them had thought. Once they finally maneuvered through the various gates while barely being able to see (not to mention steering clear of the campus patrol which maintained a strict enforcement of curfew), she pushed him out across the grassy lawn to the center of the field. As soon as she let go of his chair, she immediately dropped to the ground and lay flat on her back to look up at the stars above.

"Unbelievable!" she exclaimed with a rush of exuberance. "Brent, you've got to see this!"

Brent stared up at the dark night sky overhead. It was littered with millions of tiny sparks of light that twinkled off into a distance so far it was beyond his imagination.

"No," she told him, " you have to see it like this! Need help getting down?"

"I can manage," he answered. As much as he enjoyed her assistance, he certainly didn't want to always come across as helpless. He looked over at Abbie as she continued to stare up at the stars overhead. Even in the near total darkness, her beauty was inescapable. He quickly reached down and locked the wheels, then worked his way out of the chair and onto the lawn. She took his arm to help him anyway. He didn't mind.

She lay back down and stared upwards again. He lied down beside her and gazed up as well. She was right. It was even more amazing from this viewpoint, just looking directly up into the heavens.

"I just wish I could go up there," she whispered. "Just float among the stars. It's so peaceful."

Brent was overtaken by how wonderful it felt to just be the two of them there together, side by side. For once there was nothing else. Lying there on the grass, they were equals. He reached over and nervously took her hand.

She reacted. It wasn't a jolt or a start, just a small sensation that she felt something more than she was expecting. Or maybe it was just what she had expected after all.

She moved closer to him.

"I think I'm getting cold."

He took her in his arms and clutched her tightly. She nuzzled up next to him with her head against his. Her hair smelled so sweet.

He looked into her deep, beautiful eyes. He wanted to kiss her, but he hesitated. He shivered, but not from the cold.

"What's wrong?" she asked.

He was afraid to confess, but didn't know what he could do otherwise. "I haven't really done this before."

"It's all right," she told him. "Just take your time."

Brent stared into her eyes again for the longest time. She truly was his angel. The miracle he'd needed most in his life. He leaned closer, ever so slowly, until he finally touched her soft lips.

THE NEXT morning, Brent was a new man. Being with Abbie had already brightened his world considerably, but now there was something more. Of all people, the girl that had so tortured him as a child. And now he felt something stirring deeply within his heart.

Unfortunately, something else was in the air that morning as well. Brent overheard some of the other boys in the dormitory talking about an accident at the pool. When the Life Guards had opened up for the morning, they found a boy drowned at the bottom. No one knew how he had gotten in there. Had he snuck in overnight? How had he drowned? How did no one see him? Everyone had questions, but no one had answers.

As troubling as it was, Brent had other things on his mind. He had kissed Abbie for the first time the night before, and with every ounce of his being, he couldn't wait to see her again.

As usual, she was there waiting for him outside his dormitory. But instead of the bright smile with which she usually greeted him, she bore the same grave look of concern as everyone else he'd encountered that morning.

"Did you hear what happened?" she asked, her face full of disbelief.

"Yes," Brent replied, his joy quickly deflating. "A terrible tragedy, no doubt."

She took the handles of his wheelchair and began to push him down the sidewalk. "I've asked around," she continued, "but the University isn't talking. They won't say who it was. I'm sure they want to notify his family first."

"Yes, of course," Brent agreed solemnly.

And that was pretty much the tone for the rest of the day. Every conversation he overheard on campus was about "the boy who drowned" followed by all sorts of conjecture and theorizing about how he got in there, why the life guards hadn't seen him when locking up, and why no one had discovered him until the next morning.

It was several more days before he and Abbie spoke of what had happened that night on the field. Brent was of a mind to believe that she had dismissed the whole thing (or at least had wanted to) until she brought it up again one night outside her dormitory.

"You know, I haven't forgotten the other night," she confessed outright as she sat on the steps across from him.

"I'd hoped not," he answered. He wanted to add something else to show that he wasn't *completely* self-centered, but couldn't think of just the right words. He was tired of always sitting across from her and so wanted to be as close to her again as he was on the field. To be her equal. He reached down and locked the wheels of his chair, then grabbed the porch railing and pulled himself up.

"You need some help?" she asked, concerned.

"No, I can manage," he replied. As much as he enjoyed her assistance, this time he was determined to do it on his own. He swung himself around and landed, not as gently as he'd have liked, on the stoop next to her. Fortunately, she scooted aside just in time to keep him from landing in her lap.

"Much better," he proclaimed, as he took her hand and stared into her warm, loving eyes. "Abbie, I think I've gotten to know you better in the last month than the whole time we lived next door."

"Pretty ironic, huh?" she asked with a smile.

"Yes, definitely," he chuckled in agreement. "What I'm

trying to say is..." Brent paused, and again found himself stuck, searching for the right words. "I never thought I'd be as happy as I've been since meeting you again."

"Irony times two," she added.

"Yes, quite," he continued. "You've been the angel who brought light into my world. You rescued me from darkness in more ways than you could ever know. And the truth is, I can't imagine a second of my life without you."

"About *time* you realized it," she added.

And with that, he pulled her closer and fell into her soft kisses once again.

TWO glorious days later, Brent was on his way to class after seeing Abbie off at hers. Fortunately, her building was close by. She'd wanted to take him to class first as she usually did, but since his confession of love he was trying to be more independent. On his way, he picked up a copy of the school paper from one of the many bins that were scattered across campus. He immediately noticed Stephen's photo on the front page. He perked up at the recognition, immediately thinking that Stephen must have achieved a great honor to make the front page of the school paper. Perhaps for his performance on the swim team? Brent happily glanced at the story to quickly get the details when the realization struck him.

Stephen was the boy who had drowned in the pool.

It would not be the only funeral that he and Abbie would attend together.

CHAPTER FOURTEEN

FRANK MATSON sat in a formica-tabled booth at the Cosmic Café, eating his usual lunch of hot coffee, flapjacks, thick-cut bacon, and scrambled eggs. Frank could eat breakfast any time of day, mostly because he rarely had time to actually eat it in the morning. He was a regular at the Cosmic, so despite the fact that breakfast hours were long over, the Cook always had some extra pancake batter set aside and at the ready.

It was unusual for him to eat alone, especially lunch. Normally, he went out with one of the editors or his reporters to talk about a story. Just eating *during* lunch seemed to be a waste of valuable time.

As he doused another forkful of pancakes in a pool of syrup, he couldn't help but notice a large man in the back of the café who periodically looked up from his newspaper to watch him. The man's moustache and dark complexion told Frank that this was no coincidence. The spats on the man's shoes told him he better keep an eye on the door. "John Brown," he mumbled to himself.

After a long period of intimidating stares, Vito Spats got up from his table.

Frank glanced nervously around, his thoughts racing, wondering if the vicious killer would just gun him down right then and there. Before he had a chance to even ponder the question, Vito Spats sat down at Frank's table, directly across from him. He clutched a copy of the *Daily Crusader*.

"You work at this rag, don't you?" Vito asked.

Frank heard himself stammer a "yes," or something that sounded like one as he swallowed hard.

Vito Spats pointed to Vicky's most recent article on the O'Donnell trial. "Just reading about this trial here. Coming up soon, you know? This Victoria Rose gal you got working for you, she's a real looker." Vito Spats looked him dead in the eye for a long, hard minute, then added, "She should take care."

With that, Vito Spats got up and walked quietly out.

Frank got the message.

Loud and clear.

AS SOON as Frank got back to his desk, he called Vicky in the Press Room at City Hall and told her to get back to the office right away. She could tell by the sound of his voice that this was about more than just a progress report, even though that was the first thing he asked her.

"So, how are things going on your Nibley murder angle? And don't tell me you're not working on it any more, because I know you are. Taking more time on it than I told you, too." Frank stared her down for a moment, thinking. "So, is it a story, or not?"

Vicky looked at him, puzzled. "I thought you were against this investigation?"

Frank explained, "You don't make good reporters by telling them to ignore their hunches. You played a hunch and now it looks like you've rattled a few cages. That tells me there's a story. So, what have you got?"

Vicky perked up, "Just a lot of questions and dead ends, so far. Everything points right back to the same story, except for a few little details that don't quite add up."

"It's those details that always lead to the truth," he told her. "Stay on it, but try to keep a little quieter about it from now on. Don't want you leaving any more bloody footprints, you got me?"

The tone of Frank's voice told her that maybe this wasn't just about the car incident. "Frank, there something I ought to know?"

"Yeah," he answered with deep concern. "Certain people have taken an interest in you — certain people that you need to stay clear of. Vito Spats stopped by my table at lunch to-day to compliment your work, if you get my drift."

"Yeah, I get it," she said.

"Just be careful," he told her. Just as she was walking out, he added, chuckling, "And don't spend so much time down in the morgue, either."

That last comment caught her completely off guard. She tried to respond, if nothing else to just deny whatever he was thinking, but the words just didn't come to her. She actually found herself blushing.

WORTHINGTON was unpacking the last of his things when he heard the summoning bell. As he had for these past fifteen years, he immediately stopped what he was doing and rushed down the hall to answer. Such was the life of a manservant, a life that he was glad to continue. And that his employer had proven himself sane.

He walked into Master Brent's room and found his wheelchair in its usual spot by the window, but sitting empty. There on the small table was the hand bell. Not knowing if he should be more puzzled or concerned, Worthington called out to him. "Master Gregor? Are you there, Sir?"

As though from an invisible gust of wind, the door slammed shut behind him. Worthington turned around, startled at the noise, but saw no one there.

Worthington walked to the door and the lights went out. He felt a sudden chill in the air, as though there were a ghostly presence in there with him. He certainly wasn't alone.

"Master Gregor?" Worthington called out once more, with worry in his voice. He reached for the door knob and heard it lock by itself.

The bell rang again. Worthington turned back, but there sat the bell, still on the table. No one was near it.

Worthington grabbed the doorknob, his heart beating faster as he tried to get out. The door would not open. He was trapped.

Then came a low chuckle from the shadows in the room. Not a deep, sinister chuckle. No, it was more childish. One he'd heard many times over in years past when he had been the butt of yet another practical joke. One he hadn't heard in a very long time.

It was very comforting to hear it again.

This time he turned around slowly, not surprised to find Master Gregor seated in his wheelchair, enjoying a good laugh. Brent's ring glowed brightly.

The door unlocked itself.

Worthington straightened his coat as he settled his nerves. He tucked his fear aside and looked at Brent scornfully. "I'm sure you'll be quite the hit at your next Halloween party."

CHAPTER FIFTEEN

JUST a week later, the Harvey O'Donnell trial got underway.

If Vicky's presence at the courthouse had been less than welcome before, that had been all flowers and candy compared to the reception she received on her return.

The first inkling was her brief encounter with Chief of Police Harry LaSalle in the hallway. He smiled and tipped his hat when he saw her, then she watched his expression melt from politeness to complete disdain when the light bulb of recognition went off in his head.

"Miss Rose," he grumbled and took a quick step towards her that made her back against the wall. "What are *you* doing here?"

Vicky quickly recovered from the momentary unsettlement and stood firm as she answered, "I'm covering the O'Donnell trial. That's my job."

LaSalle let out another low grumble as he stared her down. Finally, he let out a guttural, "Right," and continued on his way.

Things didn't get any better when she made it to the press room, where Hecht and Gelbart waited, armed and ready with slings and arrows.

"So, Dollface," Hecht demanded, "I hear you've been working another angle on this O'Donnell story."

Gelbart let out a hearty laugh for good measure.

"What do you care?" Vicky shot back.

"So, you think this clown's innocent, do you?" Hecht asked

with a smirk of obvious disdain. "Listen, Sweetheart, if you want to be in the newspaper business, you can't go crying in your teacup over every poor Joe who looks like he got a raw deal. Face it, you're in the wrong place. So, go back home and bake some cookies, will you?"

Gelbart laughed again. He was a regular one-man audience.

Vicky just looked him in the eye and growled, "Out of my way, Pencil-Neck."

This time when she shoved past the two, she grabbed Gelbart's smoke, flicked it to the hardwoods and snuffed it out with the toe of her black pump. "And quit stinking up the place, Short Stuff!" she barked. "You smell like a dirty ashtray!"

The O'Donnell trial lasted almost two days. Vicky was surprised that it went on that long. Despite Frank's warnings to the contrary, she was there, front row center, as close to O'Donnell as she could get.

In the back of the courtroom sat Vito Spats. She ignored his gaze, but could feel his presence throughout the ordeal. Vito had mastered the art of intimidation.

District Attorney Everett "Doc" Milford made his opening remarks. He was well-known as a showman in the courtroom, with a shock of white hair and a penchant for tugging his suspenders when he wanted to make a point. His rotund form attested to the number of years he'd lived comfortably on Big Jack's payroll. Ever since the former D.A., Thomas Gregor, had been murdered.

Milford's statement was brief and made numerous mentions of the defendant's confession. O'Donnell's court-appointed attorney, Ed Squire, had little more to add.

The witnesses were few. Most worked for the police department, and all testified to their various roles in O'Donnell's arrest and confession. There was a quick review of the evidence — O'Donnell's fingerprints on the murder weapon and, once again, his signed confession.

Barely into the second day, the jury was sent to deliberate. Vicky heard Gelbart comment that if the jury would hurry, they could all be out before lunch. When a man's life hung in the balance, Vicky would have hated for the crowd to be inconvenienced. Perhaps they could execute him before lunch, too, she thought.

They needn't have worried. The jury returned within fifteen minutes and delivered the expected verdict. Guilty. As the Judge banged his gavel to silence the courtroom, he managed to also deliver the sentence in a timely manner. "Harvey O'Donnell, you are hereby sentenced to die in the electric chair. May God have mercy on your soul."

Vicky watched with surprise as O'Donnell bolted upright in his seat, shouting and consumed with emotion for the first time since his arrest. "The chair? But it wasn't supposed to happen this way!"

The crowd erupted again, and was barely silenced by the Judge's gavel. During the uproar, Vito Spats managed to work his way to the front of the courtroom, within eye-shot of O'Donnell.

"What do you mean, Sir?" asked the Judge. Seeing Vito Spat's stern glare, O'Donnell glanced back to his wife, Ruth. Between her pleading gaze, desperate for her husband's life, and the admonishing one from Vito Spats, O'Donnell's expression quickly changed from anger to defeat.

"Nothing, Your Honor. I'm sorry," O'Donnell replied, his head low.

With that, the Judge banged his gavel one final time. "Court is adjourned." He gathered his papers and quickly left the courtroom.

Vicky wanted to approach O'Donnell, but Vito Spats was already on him. She looked back and saw Ruth O'Donnell. Mostly, she saw the crushed look on the woman's face before being whisked out of the courtroom by two large men. They certainly didn't look like family.

BRENT wobbled carefully to his bedroom window and firmly grabbed the pane to keep himself from falling. He'd spent the last two days testing himself and his newfound abilities. He'd found that it took far greater will and concentration to force himself to walk, and even then he could only do it for short periods of time before having to fall back into his wheelchair and rest.

Much less strenuous, of course, were his other new gifts:

moving objects, turning the lights on and off, and locking and unlocking doors — all with his mind instead of his still-uncooperative body. He was sure that these skills would prove quite useful in time, but not until he could truly walk again. At the moment it was more like a cruel joke. Just enough to tempt him, but not enough to succeed.

As he struggled to continue standing, he could barely see some of the neighboring homes of Lakeview Heights in the fading sunlight. Closest, of course, was the Wentworth estate. Foremost in his mind was the burning desire to walk over there, barge in through the front doors, take Abbie in his arms and prove to her that he was finally a whole man.

But he wasn't. And Abbie wasn't there, either. She was somewhere on the other side of the world, most likely. He only hoped that she would even want to see him again.

No matter.

It was his desire to see *her* that kept him standing.

THAT NIGHT, as Vicky drove past Newsboys still hawking extras about O'Donnell's sentence, her mind was firmly locked on the story. It wasn't so much the story itself, but the thought of an innocent man being sentenced to die to cover for others. Against her better judgment, she went back to the O'Donnell apartment. She knew it was dangerous, but she had to get some answers.

Vicky looked around nervously as she stepped up to the door. It looked safe, but she knew that looks could be deceiving. She knocked quietly and waited. She was about to knock again when she spied a small face peer quickly through the curtains that covered the nearby window. Moments later, she heard cautious footsteps approach from the other side.

Ruth O'Donnell barely opened the door. It was quiet inside. Plainly furnished, but still not wanting. Clutched at her side were two boys who were too young to know, but old enough to wonder why their father wasn't coming home.

"Mrs. O'Donnell, I have to ask you a question. Why'd your husband say 'it wasn't supposed to happen this way'?" Vicky asked, carefully sliding the toe of her shoe into the door, just in case. It was a smart move. Mrs. O'Donnell tried to shut the door without answering. Vicky pleaded with her, "Please, I want to help you."

Crying, Ruth O'Donnell begged, "Please! Just go away! There's nothing you can do." She tried slamming the door again. Vicky quickly realized that she would never get any answers here and let the door close.

As she walked back to her car, she found a familiar face waiting for her. Vito Spats gave her his usual stare down. Ignoring him, she held her head high and went straight for her car. She fumbled in her purse for her keys and dropped them on the pavement.

He reached down and picked them up for her. "Allow me."

Playing the perfect gentleman, he opened her car door and handed her the keys. She looked back at him defiantly.

"Not every story has a happy ending, you know," he told her, matter-of-factly.

With her determined eyes locked on his, she shut the door and quickly drove off.

CHAPTER SIXTEEN

VICKY'D had two double chocolates at the Carousel before she finally opened up to Jerry. After all the time she'd been coming there, he knew better than to pry. She'd talk when she was good and ready. It was just about closing time, but like the good man he was, Jerry was more than willing listen.

"A man got sentenced to the chair to-day," she told him. "He's innocent, though. I know it."

"You sure?" Jerry asked as he wiped the counter top with his ever-present towel.

"As I sit here and breathe," she told him. "I've tried everything I can think of, but I just can't prove it. I just know it in my gut, that's all. But that doesn't account for much. Poor sap doesn't stand a chance."

Vicky shook her head and twirled one of the empty glasses on its edge. "It's killing me, just thinking about it. I've been through two of these already, and they haven't done me a bit of good."

"Maybe you need to hit the bar down the street," Jerry suggested, half-joking.

Vicky shrugged. "I like the company here better."

"Thanks," Jerry smiled.

"So, Bartender," Vicky continued. "You got any advice?"

Jerry leaned down on the counter in front of her. "How about if I tell you a story?"

"Sure."

"Don't know if I ever told you," Jerry began, "but I was a

pilot during the Great War. Flew quite a few missions over Germany, dropping bombs on the Krauts."

Vicky's ears perked up. She had no idea. Made her wonder even more what he was doing serving ice cream. But this was definitely not the time to ask.

"One mission, my plane got hit and the engine caught fire. The flames were blowing right back at me. We didn't get parachutes back in those days — the things were too darn heavy, and they didn't want to encourage you to turn yellow. So I only had three choices. I could jump out and end it all, I could use my revolver and end it all, or I could try to ride it down and probably burn alive on the way. Not much of a choice either way around, huh?"

Vicky just shook her head.

Jerry continued. "I was all set to jump when a thought hit me. I was still alive. And as long as I was still alive, I had a chance. Maybe not much of one, but it was still a chance."

Vicky couldn't have said anything if she'd wanted to.

"So, I rode it down. My gloves caught fire, burned the hell out of me, but I held on to that stick. I made it down, jumped out, and managed to put myself out." Jerry held out his hands. His palms were covered with faint scars from the burns. Vicky'd never noticed them before.

"As long you keep trying, you've got a chance," Jerry told her. "And I don't just mean that O'Donnell fellow, either. I'm talking about everything."

"So, how'd you end up here, dishing ice cream?" she finally had to ask.

Jerry smiled and told her, "That's a story for another night."

Vicky let Jerry's words turn over and over inside her head on the drive home. As she walked into her quiet apartment, all she could think about were the faces of those two little boys at the O'Donnell apartment earlier that night. Jerry was right. As long as O'Donnell was alive, he had a fighting chance.

And so did she.

AGAIN when Brent drifted off to sleep, he was overtaken by another rash of starkly vivid dreams. It was cold and dark. But he could walk again. And this time he could see.

Brent ventured through the rock-covered and heavily wooded landscape. He heard the faint cries of someone in the far distance. He examined his clothing — he was dressed all in black, with a large, flowing cloak, a wide-brimmed hat, and a long, scarlet head scarf beneath it. Covering his face was a mask.

He pulled the glove from his right hand. On his finger was the ring with the fiery red opal. It glowed brightly.

Ahead of him on the ground was a puddle of water. He rushed over to it and looked down. The mask he wore was decorated with a gleaming white skull.

He heard the cries again.

Pulling the glove back on, he rushed onward into the darkness, and found himself being pulled into the shadows where he could not be seen. On the road up ahead he saw them. An older woman, dressed in rags, lay in the mud, reaching up and crying. A large, well-dressed and brutish man had a young girl, no more than sixteen, with his arm around her neck, and was dragging her off.

"Please, leave my daughter, she is all I have!" cried the woman. Though Brent could not speak her language, he understood her words.

"Stop!" Brent shouted.

The man did as he was commanded. He looked up, but saw no one else there. "Who goes there?" asked the man. "Come out where I can see you!"

Brent was on him in an instant. He knocked the man to the ground, freeing the daughter, who quickly ran to her mother's side.

The brutish man struggled back to his feet, but still saw no sign of his attacker.

"Go." Brent commanded the woman and her daughter. They looked back, just as puzzled, then hurried away.

"Come back here, you!" shouted the man. He lunged after them, but was pummeled once again by an unseen force. This time when he looked up, he saw a figure, a black spectre, that glowered over him. The woman and her daughter saw it too, then prayed to God before disappearing into the night.

Fear gripped the man as he scurried back, clawing at the ground to escape the ghostly image before him.

WHITEY O'LEARY had sat in his car outside the Belmont Hotel since before dawn. He had three other men positioned in cars at various points around the block, all heavily armed with shotguns. This time, he was determined to take down Vito Spats and there would be *no* escape.

He looked upstairs to the sixth floor. He'd placed a man in the hotel a month ago to watch Vito Spats' every move. He knew what time Spats left and what time he returned. And on this particular morning his lookout would wave a white kerchief from the window to let him know when Spats was on his way down.

Whitey anxiously checked his watch again. Spats was later than usual. Probably still upstairs with his beautiful young wife (and who could blame him?). It didn't matter. It was only a matter of time. Whitey had been patient. And this time it would pay off. He was sure of it.

Finally, the signal came. The white kerchief fluttered at the window high above. Whitey chuckled at the thought of Vito Spat's final surrender.

Whitey got out of the car, his shotgun tucked carefully into his coat. It was too warm to wear such a long coat, but he didn't want to take any chances on being noticed too soon.

Whitey gave the nod for each of his men to follow. They all got out of their cars, careful to keep their guns out of sight too, just as he had done.

As they watched the door, ready to move, a black and white Patrol Car drove by the front of the hotel and paused for a moment. Whitey's expression dropped. After all this time, all his patience, he wasn't about to let this chance get away.

His expression dropped even more when the Patrol Car pulled up to the curb and parked. Whitey looked to see that one of his men, "Nags," had parked in front of a hydrant. Of all the luck.

And what was worse, Nags was standing right by it with a shotgun tucked in his coat. Nags backed nonchalantly away from the car and looked into a neighboring store window. His side hiding the shotgun was turned away from the Cop.

Whitey's men looked to him for an answer. Whitey thought for a moment, then nodded towards the hotel to signal that they were going ahead. If the Cop got in their way, so be it. That was the way it had to be. He nodded to Nags to take him out. He couldn't chance it otherwise.

The tall, stocky Policeman got out of his cruiser with his citation book. Whitey checked him over. The Cop was armed. But his holster was snapped. The Cop looked at the car, then over at Nags.

"This your car?" the Cop asked.

"No, Sir," Nags answered. "I was just walking here."

The Cop eyed him suspiciously then looked back to the car.

Whitey's eyes stayed locked on the hotel doors.

He saw some shadows move about inside the lobby. The Doorman stepped out and opened the door.

Spats' current driver, "Willie Potatoes," walked out first. It was time to move.

Whitey clutched his shotgun inside his coat and started across the street. The Policeman put his foot on the bumper of the car as he wrote the citation.

Then Vito Spats walked out of the hotel surrounded by two more of his men.

Whitey couldn't get a clear shot. He looked to the man on his left, "Monk" McCarthy, Nails' younger brother. Monk shook his head. Whitey hesitated.

It was no good.

Should they scram? He wondered. But there was no way they could leave without being seen.

He hadn't come this far just to quit. They had him surrounded.

Whitey whipped out his shotgun and opened fire.

He hit Willie in the shoulder, but he didn't take him down.

The Doorman dove for the sidewalk.

Spats and his men ducked for the Police Cruiser and reached for their guns. As did the Cop.

Nags unloaded on the Cop. He went right down, his pistol still stuck in his holster.

Willie Potatoes hit Nags in the kneecap, then again in the chest. Nags should have worried about him before the Cop.

Whitey and his remaining men attempted to circle in on Spats. They blasted out all the windows of the Black and White. But for all the lead they spent, they just couldn't connect with their target.

Spats' men fired back in all directions to gain some cover. Spats dove for the hotel doors. The Doorman tried to follow and caught a shot in the leg.

Whitey blasted after him, but it was no good. He'd have to chase Spats through the hotel to finish him off.

He shook his head in frustration, then signaled his men back to their cars. They'd missed their chance.

And taken out a Cop in the process.

There would be hell to pay.

CHAPTER SEVENTEEN

BRENT stared at the dull ring on his finger all morning. It had glowed brightly when he'd first put it on, but now it had been at least two days since he'd seen it even flicker. The initial power that the ring had granted had worn off, and now he was fast becoming a cripple once more. Previously, he'd been able to nearly walk across the room, but now he could barely get out of his chair. Frustrated, he attempted it again.

Gripping the handles of his wheelchair, he lifted himself up to a standing position. Legs shaking, he vainly tried to take a step towards the bed. It was no use. He soon felt himself falling and crumbled to the floor with a loud thud. He looked for his bell on the table, but needn't have worried. Worthington rushed in to help.

"Master Gregor! Oh, dear!" Worthington lifted him under the arms, still strong for an aging man, and hoisted him back in the wheelchair. He even managed to do it without dropping the morning paper, which he'd tucked under his arm.

"Just so frustrating, Worthington," Brent grumbled, his ire getting the best of him. "I really believed this was the answer!" Angrily, Brent grabbed the nearest book and threw it across the room.

"As did I, Sir," Worthington responded, going to pick up the book. Brent knew it was a lie, but Worthington was so polite and loyal, it was nearly convincing. Worthington handed Brent the morning paper, promising to return with breakfast momentarily.

His patience exhausted, Brent wheeled himself over to the window. How he wanted to leave this house! This prison! To do something for himself and not have to depend on Worthington for every little thing. Every previous attempt to walk had met nothing but failure. And now it appeared that this one had too.

Brent glanced down at the newspaper that Worthington had given him. The headline was a carry-over from yesterday's Extra. "O'DONNELL GETS THE CHAIR," by Victoria Rose. The name instantly rang a bell. He remembered the headstrong young reporter standing there in a nurse's uniform, pleading with him. "An innocent man could be executed! I need your help to serve justice!"

Then he remembered the words of Madame Ouspenskaya, "You must bring justice to those who have none." If he was going to get out of that chair again, he had to act.

Brent spoke up just as Worthington reached the door. "Worthington, I need you to call this Victoria Rose and invite her up to the house."

"Yes, indeed, Sir," his Manservant answered.

VICKY was practically singing when she phoned Denny down in the morgue to tell him the good news. "That's right, Brent Gregor called *me*. Actually, it was his butler, but that's what rich guys do. Can you believe it?"

Denny was stunned. Vicky excitedly told him that she was going to meet Gregor at his mansion. "I'm heading over there right now. Maybe he finally wants to help after all. I wonder what changed his mind?" she pondered.

"Well, if he's smart," Denny answered, "it was the chance to see you again."

There was a moment of awkward silence on the phone, and Denny wished he hadn't let that comment out so quickly.

Vicky spoke up first. "Actually, I've been thinking about that. That invitation for dinner still open?"

Denny was surprised. He was glad that this was a phone conversation so that she couldn't see all the color leave his face. "I, uh, thought you just wanted to keep things on a...

professional level?" he asked.

"Yes, I did," she answered. "But certain events lately have made me rethink a lot of things. Life's just too short, you know. So, where you want to go?"

Again, Denny regretted his answer right after he blurted it out. "Vicedomini's?"

"Wow, you don't mess around, do you?"

That was just the response he feared. Just when she was starting to warm up to him, he was about to scare her back off. His choice of restaurant threw her for a quick loop. Vicedomini's was the most romantic restaurant in town. Where men always take their girlfriends when they're ready to propose. He hadn't suggested it to be forward, though. In actuality, his uncle was the Maitre d' and it was the only nice restaurant in town where he knew he could get a good table on such short notice.

"We can go somewhere else if you like," Denny stuttered, sure he'd be dining alone now.

"Well, actually," she began, and Denny knew it was coming. "I don't know how long I'll be at the Gregor Mansion, so how about if I meet you there. Six o'clock sound good?"

"Swell," Denny replied, too enthusiastically, but he just couldn't help it. She could hear him smiling clear through the phone line. "Good luck!" He sounded like a schoolboy getting his first date, which wasn't too far off from the truth, but he was far too excited to care.

WHITEY O'LEARY and Monk McCarthy sped nervously down 112th Street. They'd already been to Whitey's hotel and called Nails McCarthy with the bad news. Their plan was to get out of town, head south and just lay low for a time.

It was bad enough that they'd failed yet again to get Vito Spats, but this time they'd taken out a Cop, too. Nails was none too happy about it. But what was worse, the entire Terminal City police force was out looking to get evens. They protected their own more viciously than a mother lion.

And Whitey's luck had long run out.

He just didn't know it yet.

"I'm telling you, Monk, everything's gonna be Aces," Whitey reassured him. "You just drive to the station and let me do the worryin', okay?"

"Yeah, okay," Monk replied as he white-knuckled the steering wheel with sweaty palms. He wouldn't be ready to rest easy until they were on that train headed due south.

As Monk turned wildly down Colfax, they passed a Police Cruiser that was out looking for the killers. And they just happened to match the description.

If Monk had been smart, he would have slowed down and played it cool. But Monk just wasn't that smart.

He gunned the motor and sped up. That got the Cops' attention. They slammed on brakes and spun their cruiser around in the street to take up the chase.

"Nuts!" Whitey shouted. "Gun it! Gun it!"

Monk roared down Colfax and masterfully whipped the car around between the streetcars and oncoming traffic. But it wasn't enough. The police cruiser stayed right on their tail and didn't let up. For block after block, the police car kept right behind them with sirens blaring.

Monk saw his chance with an approaching streetcar and a line of cars parked at a red light ahead. If he could just squeeze through, the Cops would be stopped in their tracks. He rammed the gas pedal into the floor and swerved into the fast-closing space. Whitey gripped the dashboard and said a quiet Ave Maria. If they lived, it would be a narrow escape. It was too late to protest.

Monk's heart stopped at the sound of clashing metal when their car connected with the streetcar. He held his breath and waited for the full impact, but they just scraped along the side and burst out the other side like a newborn from the birth canal. They both let out a joyous sigh of relief as the Cops slammed on brakes and skidded sideways in the street, narrowly avoiding being crushed themselves.

Monk down-shifted and hit the gas again to pick up speed. The Cops were stuck long enough for them to get away.

"Murder! That was close!" Whitey exclaimed.

"And how!" Monk agreed and wiped the sweat from his brow. But he should have paid more attention to the road ahead. If he had, he would have noticed the large garbage truck that turned off a side street directly in front of them.

"Rats!" Monk shouted as he whipped the steering wheel and slammed on brakes. The car went into a skid and slid around backwards before it crashed into a light pole next to a vacant lot. Whitey and Monk were thrown forward by the impact. Monk's chest took the full force of it when he slammed into the steering wheel.

Whitey looked up, his face bloodied from the broken side window and where his head had smacked into the windshield.

"Monk, you okay?" Whitey asked.

Monk was slumped over and gasped for breath. Whitey sat him up to help him catch his breath.

"Come on, Pal!" Whitey told him. "We gotta get outa here!"

Still gasping for breath, Monk fumbled for his pistol. Whitey already had his ready. It was a good thing, because before they could even get out they were staring down the police cruiser with its lights still flashing, the siren still blaring, and two officers armed with pistols and bearing down on them.

Whitey chuckled at the situation as he reached into the back to grab a pair of Tommy guns. On the surface, it didn't look good. But despite their injuries, they had the Cops outgunned. The officers wouldn't expect them to come out shooting. Especially while they played 'possum. It was the perfect plan.

Or at least it seemed so at the time.

CHAPTER EIGHTEEN

THE TWO Detectives armed with shotguns that got out of the back seat of the police cruiser should have changed his mind. But they didn't. Whitey was determined to come out fighting.

"Come on, out of the car! Both of you!" shouted the larger of the two Detectives.

Whitey kept his head low as he watch the Detectives approach. Monk did the same, though he still struggled for breath.

"Just keep down till I give the go-ahead," Whitey told him.

Monk could only manage a slight nod.

Whitey was sure it would work.

With no movement from the car, the Detectives moved closer still. Just as it looked like it might be safe, Whitey and Monk sat up and opened fire through what was left of the broken windshield. Both Detectives went down as a barrage of gunfire hit them square in the chest.

The uniformed officers dove for the pavement as Whitey and Monk opened fire on them and sprayed their car with a hail of bullets. Broken glass from the windshield and siren rained down on them like a torrential downpour.

Whitey charged his prey and opened fire again on the officer closest to him. The poor man was a sitting duck. Whitey riddled his body with bullets while the remaining officer rolled under the car for protection.

As soon as he stopped shooting, the air was filled with

the sound of approaching sirens. They were coming fast. Whitey shouted for them to make tracks and beat it.

"Come on! This way!" Whitey called to Monk as he barreled across the vacant lot. Monk followed behind and struggled to keep up.

As soon as Whitey and Monk were on the run, the lone officer scrambled from beneath the car. He rushed to retrieve the shotguns from the fallen Detectives and quickly gave chase.

Monk spotted the officer and launched a volley of gunfire from his Tommy gun. But his gun jammed and the officer ducked quickly before opening fire himself with a shotgun. He hit Monk clean in the leg just above the knee. Monk let out a shriek of pain before falling to the pavement now stained with his own blood. Whitey looked back in shock to see it spurt from Monk's gaping wound.

Whitey let loose a barrage of gunfire himself that sent the officer down face-first.

"Come on!" he shouted, then grabbed Monk by the arm. He practically dragged him the rest of way until they were able to safely duck into a nearby residential alley.

They ran a good distance until Monk just couldn't go any further. His face was ashen white. The trail of blood he'd left behind clearly answered why. The lone officer's shotgun blast had punctured an artery and Monk would be lucky if he were to live much longer.

"You gotta get outa here," Monk told him. "Don't worry about me. I ain't gonna make it anyway."

Whitey wanted to disagree, but his street-honed survival instincts got the better of him. He couldn't just leave him there for the Cops and looked around anxiously.

"Here," Whitey said and rushed down a small stairwell to a nearby basement. He tried the door, but it was locked. Not to be deterred, he busted out a ground-level window with the butt of his Tommy gun. He cleared away the jagged glass and then helped Monk crawl through and drop down to the floor below.

With his friend now tucked away out of sight, Whitey said a quick Ave Maria and raced off down the alley.

Monk lay on the floor for what seemed like an eternity

until the door was finally smashed in. He looked up weakly to see the lone officer walk in with his shotgun drawn and ready. Behind him were three more armed officers.

They needn't have bothered.

Monk lay in a heap, barely clinging to life in a dark pool of glass and blood. The lone officer rushed upstairs just as quickly as he had entered to call for an ambulance.

Monk was dead before they ever reached the hospital.

WORTHINGTON led Vicky down the long hallway, just as he had done on her last visit. Though she wasn't attempting to play a ruse this time, she was still just as nervous as before. "I'm still sorry about the last time I was here," Vicky confided.

"No need to worry, Miss," Worthington answered. "I hoped we would meet again under better circumstances, and it appears that we have."

Worthington gave a quick knock on the door, then swung it open and led her in. Just as before, Brent Gregor sat in his wheelchair by the window. Beside him on the small table was a large envelope. There was also an empty chair. Though still stern, he seemed more welcoming and agreeable this time.

"May I get you anything, Miss? A glass of wine, perhaps?" Worthington asked. Vicky instinctively refused, then quickly wondered when she'd have another opportunity where a Butler offered her wine while visiting such a grand mansion. "Actually, yes, that would be lovely," she told him. "Whatever you suggest."

"Of course, Miss Rose," Worthington said as he bowed and dismissed himself.

Brent attempted to offer a friendly smile. "Miss Rose, so good to see you again. Please, sit down." He directed her to the empty chair, then continued, "I wish to apologize for my behavior on your last visit. It was rude of me."

Vicky blushed as she sat with him. "You don't have to apologize to me, Mr. Gregor. I'm the one who barged in here uninvited, pretending to be a nurse. Actually, it's a good thing you found me out before we got to your shot. I never did get the hang of that."

Brent smiled warmly, proving that he could actually do it. "I was going to make sure that you didn't. Still, I do wish to apologize. Fifteen years in a wheelchair can make a man bitter, but that's no excuse for my actions, just the truth about them."

Vicky looked at him, puzzled. Such a pleasant man, she thought. So different from the one she had met before.

She then took notice of the aged, ornate ring on his finger. It seemed so unlikely a decoration for a man who's room had virtually none. She couldn't help but be puzzled by it. Especially that he hadn't worn it before. She was certain that if he had, she would have noticed it already.

"That's an interesting ring," she remarked.

Brent answered quickly. "Thank you. It's something I recently inherited."

The patch of silence that followed told her undoubtedly that this was all he would say about it.

"I have to confess," she interjected, "I was really surprised to get your call. What did you want to see me about?"

Brent told her, "A few years ago, I hired a private detective, Sam Donohue was his name, to find out if Ned Vogel is really insane. Donohue was supposed to meet Worthington one night down near the train station and deliver a package. But he never showed. The next day, he was found in the river, a bullet to the back of the head."

Vicky grimaced at the thought. Worthington breezed in silently and delivered a glass of white wine to her. "Thank you," she told him as he drifted back out just as quietly.

Brent continued, "A few days later, I got this package in the mail." He tapped the large envelope on the table between them. "It was everything Donohue had found so far. I've read through it several times, but I've never been able to find anything special." He handed it to Vicky. "Perhaps with what you know, you can."

Vicky anxiously set down her wine glass, staring at the still-sealed envelope. She looked at the postmark — 1933. Three years earlier.

"Go ahead," Brent told her. "You can open it."

Using her nails, she quickly broke the seal on the flap and pulled out a stuffed file folder. She opened it straight away and glanced through its contents. The top layer was a good number of newspaper clippings, all of the articles that she and Denny had recently read pertaining to Thomas Gregor's murder, Ned Vogel's trial and commitment to the asylum, Sarah Gregor's illness and her obituary. Below the clippings was a batch of official documents, most of them documents pertaining to the news stories. One in particular caught her eye, though. It was Ned's commitment papers.

Perusing through them, she found something else that grabbed her attention. "Wait a minute," she asked, "Who was the doctor at Ned's trial who testified that he was insane?"

Brent answered without even having to think. "Dr. Kobler." Even after all these years, he still had the details firmly etched in his mind. Even more vividly etched were the memories of going to visit his mother in that dreaded asylum. Every Sunday, Worthington would push his small chair out of the house and load him into the car. Brent could still hear Julius Kennelly's taunting laughter at the sight of "the little crippled boy going to visit his crazy mother." Young Brent's heart grew to learn true hatred. He wanted to lash out at Julius, but all he could ever do was cry. Worthington always told him to be strong and to hold his head high. Brent long wondered if Worthington ever felt pain, or if he were just numb to the world around him. At his young age, he could never understand Worthington's stoicism or the pain he had felt in years past.

Vicky's voice stirred him quickly back to the present when she asked, "Then why are his commitment papers signed by Dr. Hyneman?"

Brent looked up at her, puzzled. "Who's Dr. Hyneman?"

Vicky told him, "He's the psychiatrist who runs the asylum. I think this just might be the key to unlocking the whole case."

Brent watched the wheels turn inside Vicky's head before she was finally able to relay the details. "I think I've finally figured it all out. O'Donnell didn't kill the Mayor, Ned Vogel did. And he's not insane, either. They just keep up the ruse because it's the perfect cover. A rock-solid alibi. They paid O'Donnell a nice sum to claim he did it, told him he'd only have to do a little time to protect his family, then they rigged the evidence. Only O'Donnell didn't realize they'd double-cross him, so now he's going to the chair, and they all get off scot-free. All neat and tidy."

Before Brent could even respond, Vicky jumped to her feet and thanked him. "May I take this?" she asked. Brent only managed a nod before she started for the door, then swung back on her heel and tossed back the rest of her wine. Then she kissed him on the cheek and whirled out the door, brushing past Worthington like a brewing whirlwind just picking up steam.

"Well," Worthington quipped, "I see that conversation went better than your previous encounter."

As Worthington went to retrieve the empty wine glass, he took notice of Brent's ring. "Master, your ring!"

Brent looked down to see the ring glowing brighter than it had ever done before, though he didn't need Worthington to call his attention to it. He could already feel its strength course through him. He quickly gripped the handles of his chair and lifted himself to a standing position.

"Master, are you sure?" Worthington asked.

"As sure as I've ever been," Brent answered confidently. Steeling his courage, he took a confident step away from his chair and found himself still standing. Worthington could only watch in wide-eyed amazement. Eager for this regained strength to continue, Brent stepped to the window and watched as Vicky jumped in her car and sped off.

"You must bring justice to those who have none."

CHAPTER NINETEEN

VICKY waited impatiently in the lobby at the Asylum. The Desk Nurse was rather relieved when Dr. Hyneman came out. She was getting tired of hearing Vicky's heals clack against the usually serene tiled floor as she paced back and forth.

"Miss Rose?" Dr. Hyneman asked. "To what do I owe the honor of another visit?" Vicky told him that she had a few more questions regarding Three-Finger Ned Vogel. The tone in her voice told him quite clearly that this was not a conversation to be had in the open. In true gentlemanly fashion, he invited her back to his office.

"I can assure you that Mr. Vogel is without a doubt, certifiably insane," Dr. Hyneman assured her when Vicky expressed her doubts.

Vicky wasn't going to fall for it and came back with both barrels, "Then why didn't you testify at Ned's trial, instead of Dr. Kobler? Dr. Kobler never even treated Vogel."

Dr. Hyneman looked back at her sternly, confused about just how to answer and still maintain his friendly pretense. "I'm afraid I don't know what you're talking about."

"Yes, you do," Vicky shot back. "I want to see Vogel right now. Right this instant."

Dr. Hyneman responded firmly, "No, the patients cannot be disturbed at this hour. Perhaps if you come back in the morning."

Feeling herself so close to the truth, Vicky let her zeal get the best of her. "No, I'm going to see him now." She pushed past him and bolted down the hall. She rushed up the first staircase to get to Ned's room. Dr. Hyneman ran back to his office and called the Orderly desk, praying that they could intercept her before she got there. But even in heels, Vicky was fast and more than that, she was determined.

Vicky practically slid to a stop at Ned's door and burst straight into the room. It's hard to say who was more surprised – her or them. Ned was seated at a table with a cigar in his mouth, playing cards with two other "patients." All three men were in their pajamas, in a room decorated with cigar smoke, empty gin bottles, and a lewd calendar for the Terminal City Tire Company. Even though it was better than what she expected, she was still surprised. It was too bad she didn't have her camera.

Ned's shocked look immediately switched to a big grin. "Hey Doll, nice of you to drop in." The other two turned around with lascivious smiles, happy to see a woman who wasn't a nurse.

Vicky gave Ned a victorious smile as she sauntered over to him triumphantly. "Ned Vogel, you don't know how happy I am to see you."

"Oh, yeah?" Vogel answered, his mind going way off in the wrong direction. "You don't know how happy I am to see you. But I'll be glad to show youse!" Ned and his boys got a good chuckle until the moment when two large Orderlies rushed in, followed by a very concerned Dr. Hyneman. "Oops," Ned muttered.

Vicky continued the thought, "Oops is right." Now that she had her story, she had to get out of there fast. Outrunning the Orderlies would be a problem. Getting past them would be a bigger problem.

Vicky was a fast thinker, though, and before any of them could contemplate their next move, she already had her perfume bottle out of her purse. She sprayed it straight at Vogel, catching a spark from the end of his cigar and catching his shirt lightly ablaze. The move bought her just enough time to break for the door, but she hadn't counted on the brick wall that was standing on the other side.

A brick wall named Vito Spats. "Miss Rose. I can't tell you how disappointed I am to see you here."

Vicky dropped her perfume bottle as Vito Spats gripped her around both arms with his large hands like a human vice. She tried kicking him, but it was no use. As many had discovered long before her, once you were into Vito Spats' grasp, there was no escape.

Vito pushed a struggling Vicky down the hall, into the elevator, and back to Dr. Hyneman's office. Needing to keep her secure and where she couldn't cause any more trouble than she already had, he shoved her in the closet and locked the door.

Finding every loose paper and shelf as she stumbled back to her feet in the dark, Vicky went straight for the door, hoping to catch whatever bits of conversation that she could from the other side. The only thing worse than being locked in that closet would have been to miss anything being said in Dr. Hyneman's office.

"What are we going to do with her?" asked Dr. Hyneman, clearly worried.

Vito Spats replied matter-of-factly. "Just keep her quiet 'til I get back. I gotta do something about her car. Think you can handle that?"

DENNY sat at the restaurant table, waiting nervously and drumming his fingers on the checkered table cloth. He'd gotten there a half-hour early just to make sure his uncle didn't give his table away, and to make a good impression. By this point, he'd studied every detail of the Old World Italian décor and been through two baskets of bread slices and three plates of olive oil and sautéed garlic.

His uncle, Edward Morris, stopped by his table. "Denny, I'm sorry to say, but I just don't think the young lady is coming." As much as he wanted Denny to have a date, it seemed painfully true by this point. Had Denny come to him for advice, he would have suggested another restaurant.

"Just a little longer, Uncle Edward," Denny told him. His uncle shook his head and went to retrieve another basket of bread.

Vicky was an hour late already and his mind had already raced through a number of scenarios. For the first twenty minutes that she didn't show, he felt that he'd been too forward suggesting Vicedomini's and that she'd changed her mind. For the second twenty minutes, he was convinced that she wanted absolutely nothing to do with him and that this was just her way of humiliating him to make the point, and he was only humiliating himself even further by staying. During the third twenty minutes, he worried that perhaps something had happened to her, felt guilty for the first two scenarios, and thought that even if she had stood him up, he should call to make sure she was all right.

Denny went to the phone booth in the back and quickly deposited his nickel. "Operator, could you connect me to Mrs. Hershey's Boarding House for Women?"

Denny nervously drummed his fingers on the window of the booth as he waited for the call to go through. Finally, with a short crackle, he heard Mrs. Hershey's elderly voice on the other line. "Yes?"

"Hello, I'm trying to reach Miss Vicky Rose. Is she there, please?" he asked anxiously.

"Is this a gentleman caller?" Mrs. Hershey inquired sternly.

While he hoped that he certainly was, Denny quickly surmised that being so might not be the best tactic. "No ma'am," he fibbed, "this is, uh... Mr. Morris. I work with Miss Rose at the *Crusader*. I need to speak with her if I can."

"Well, she's not here," replied Mrs. Hershey, suspicious that a co-worker would be calling the boarding house rather than Miss Rose's apartment directly. Denny barely got out a thank-you before she said "good day" and hung up on him.

Denny stood silently in the booth for a few moments, his body still but his mind racing. He was relieved to know that perhaps she hadn't stood him up after all, but at this point he was even more convinced that something was wrong. It was at that point that his mind replayed their last conversation. She was going to the Gregor Mansion. That was the last thing he knew. Denny grabbed the phone again.

"Operator, could you connect me with the Gregor Mansion please?"

He waited anxiously for someone to answer. Anyone. Finally, on the sixth ring, the voice of a kindly, English gentleman came on the line. "Gregor Mansion. How may I be of service?"

"Hi," Denny stuttered. "This is Denny Morris with the *Daily Crusader*." He thought he'd have better luck if he tried to sound official again. "I'm trying to find Vicky Rose. She was supposed to meet with Mr. Gregor earlier. Is she still there by any chance?"

Worthington responded, "Yes, Miss Rose was here earlier, but she left some time ago. Is there a problem?"

Denny resumed his anxious tapping on the wall of the booth. "That's just it, I don't know. She was supposed to meet me for dinner an hour ago. I'm just a little worried, that's all. Did she say if she was going anywhere else?"

"Perhaps you should speak with Master Gregor," Worthington replied. Denny was too nervous to speak with Brent Gregor himself, but Worthington put down the phone before he could tell him that it wasn't necessary.

Denny was just about to hang up when Brent Gregor's strong and determined voice came on the line. "Hello, this is Brent Gregor. What can I do for you?"

Denny did his best not to trip over his words. "Uh, hi, Mr. Gregor. I'm so sorry to bother you. My name is Denny Morris and I work with Vicky, I mean, Miss Rose, at the *Crusader*. She's late for a, uh, dinner meeting, and I was just getting a little worried, that's all. I'm really sorry if I'm interrupting anything."

"No, not at all," Brent answered. "I'm sure she'd appreciate your concern. Actually, she left a couple of hours ago. We were talking about a story. She didn't say where she was going, but..." Brent thought for a moment. "She may have gone by the Asylum. I would check with them."

"Thank you so much, Mr. Gregor," Denny said. "So sorry to bother you."

"Think nothing of it. Thank you for calling," Brent said as he hung up.

Denny set down the receiver and tapped on the wall again. The more he thought about it, the more worried he became. Perhaps something did happen to her? She'd certainly made a lot of enemies lately. But what could he do? Probably nothing much, but he'd never forgive himself if something did happen and he just sat idly by and did nothing about it.

Denny bolted from the booth and shouted a quick thank you to his uncle on his way out the door. Uncle Edward shook his head again as he returned to the kitchen with the third basket of bread.

BRENT GREGOR tapped nervously on the arm of his wheelchair. Vicky Rose had left his house over two hours ago, and was supposed to have met that man for dinner. She'd made a lot of enemies recently. Could something have happened to her? What could he do about it? He could barely walk. And he'd sworn that he would never go back to that dreadful place again.

He looked at the ring on his finger. It was starting to glow deep from within.

"Bring justice to those who have none."

The thought echoed in the back of his mind. With it, too, was the thought of Vicky Rose. If the worst were to happen, he would never be able to live with himself.

Brent rang for Worthington. "Worthington, I need you to get the car. We're going to the Asylum."

"The Asylum, Sir?" Worthington asked, shocked beyond words.

"Yes," Brent answered emphatically. "I think something may have happened to Miss Rose."

"Shouldn't we call the police, Sir?" asked Worthington.

Brent shook his head. "I would if I knew who we could trust. I'm afraid we're going to have to tackle this one on our own."

Brent gave Worthington a determined look, then gripped the handles of his wheelchair. Before Worthington could voice another objection, Brent was on his feet. Steeling his resolve, he stepped forward. With a few clumsy first steps and slowly increasing agility, he walked straight up to Worthington.

Brent felt the strength within him continue to build. He looked down at his hand. The ring was glowing brighter than ever before. Both of them were astounded by its luminescence.

Smiling triumphantly, Brent said, "Worthington, I need you to bring me that box."

CHAPTER TWENTY

AS THEY rode down in the elevator, Vicky struggled against the leather straps that bound her to a wheeled gurney, but it was to no avail. She was fastened securely as Ned and Billy Turkle, one of the other "patients" she saw playing cards, wheeled her quickly down the hallway. She was also gagged — a firm leather harness was around her head that included a thick leather strap between her teeth. It prevented her from screaming. She didn't want to think of the reason why.

Vicky had been in some tough spots before, but this was by far the worst. She worried she had done just as Frank had feared and finally tread too far this time.

Thinking feverishly, she pondered any possible means of escape. It looked hopeless. Try as she might, there was no way to get loose from the gurney. And even if she did, she still had to contend with Vito Spats, Ned, and who knows how many others? She would need more than just her usually quick mind and handy luck to get out of this one. She would need help, and she couldn't possibly see where any was forthcoming.

Who would even know where to look for her? Certainly not Frank. Denny would be the first to notice she was gone, but what could he do? Brent Gregor was the only person who even knew where she might be.

Trying not to lose hope, she remembered Jerry's words. "As long as you're alive, you have a chance." She kept repeating that mantra over and over in her mind in between her prayers. It was the only thing that kept her going.

As they got off the elevator on the basement level, Ned and Turkle pushed the table on which Vicky lay through a set of secure double doors at the end of a long hallway. Two large Orderlies stood guard outside.

Vicky was momentarily disoriented as they spun her around and moved her table into position. As she looked up to take in her surroundings, she caught sight of Dr. Hyneman readying a bank of strange electrical equipment clearly designed for patient submission. None of them paid any attention to her muted protestations, whether they heard them or not.

She was almost relieved when Vito Spats barged into the room, showing signs that he was clearly not happy with what was about to happen. However, it was poor comfort indeed.

"What are you doing down here, Doc?" he demanded. "I got orders to bump her off."

Vicky looked up at Vito Spats with pleading eyes. Her hopes dwindling, she prayed for sympathy. Though a quick gunshot to the head was certainly preferable to what she was obviously about to experience.

Dr. Hyneman turned to him calmly and answered, "I promise you, that won't be necessary."

"But she knows too much," argued Vito Spats.

Dr. Hyneman reassured him. "Exactly. I haven't been sitting here idly at this Asylum for all these years. I've been developing a new system of electroshock therapy. By applying jolts of electricity to certain areas of her brain, I can make Miss Rose forget everything she knows about the past –– from days, to weeks, to even months. It's all in how I apply the electricity. How high the voltage and to which parts of the brain. It's very useful for patients who have experienced great trauma, or for patients who just need to forget. It's quite effective, I assure you."

"That's got to be real painful," mumbled Turkle with surprise.

"Immensely," smirked Dr. Hyneman as he leered down at Vicky. "And the side effects are crippling. Trust me, she'll end up in my care for the rest of her short life."

Vicky struggled again against the straps. Tears streamed down her cheeks. The gag prevented her from screaming out loud. She hoped that maybe there was some humanity in one of them, but was sure that it was an empty wish.

Vito Spats nodded, still unsure and unconvinced. "Okay, but if it don't work, I'm gonna bump her off anyways."

Dr. Hyneman signaled to Ned and Turkle. They wheeled her over to the waiting equipment. Vicky looked with terrified eyes at the mass of thick cables that ran from the wall to the equipment before her. More cables ran to a steel contraption that was clearly designed to fit over her head. Again, Vicky screamed as loud as she could through the leather gag. The men all laughed as she struggled against her bindings.

Dr. Hyneman leaned over her, smiling. "Go ahead, Miss Rose. Scream all you want. There will be a lot more screaming to come. No one can hear you down here. And even if they did, no one cares about screams coming from an asylum."

Vito, Ned, and Turkle watched skeptically as Dr. Hyneman worked to set up the equipment. "Prepare to witness the marvel of modern science."

BRENT had Worthington pull the car over by the rear grounds of the Asylum. The entire property was surrounded by a high, wrought iron fence with barbed wire at the top. He knew these grounds far to well. All those years of visiting his mother and watching her go slowly insane. If there were ever any place to which he never wanted to return, this was surely it. He feared it more than the Patterson House.

"Pull up as close to the fence as you can," Brent told him.

"Are you certain of this, Master Gregor?" Worthington asked, betraying his own sense of fear. Years of service had finally dimmed his rock-solid stoicism.

"Yes, I'm sure," Brent answered.

Worthington did just as he'd been instructed, careful not to get too close and scratch the car. It wasn't damaging the vehicle he was concerned about as much as not wanting to leave any evidence that they had been there.

Turning away from the wretched memories that haunted him, Brent stared at the box in his lap. He tugged at the thin leather strap that held the lid in place and pulled it away. Inside was a wide-brimmed black hat and a long, blood red head scarf like a Gypsy would wear. Beneath the hat was a black cloak and a pair of black leather gloves.

Brent turned the hat over and found something that gave him a start when he first saw it. It was a mask that covered the whole head. On it was painted the top portion of a skull. He remembered it from his dream. He reached into the hat to pick it up.

As soon as he touched the fabric, memories of having worn it before came rushing back to him. Mercifully, they clouded out the memories he had for so long wished to erase. He sat there quietly, unmoving, for several minutes before Worthington finally asked, "Master Gregor, are you all right, Sir?"

Brent snapped back to the present. "Yes, Worthington. I'm fine." It was all clear to him now. He knew what he had to do. "Worthington, I need you to wait here. I'm going inside to look for Miss Rose."

"But, Sir," Worthington pleaded, "are you sure about this?"

"Yes," Brent insisted. "Wait for twenty minutes, then go to the nearest phone, call the Fire Department, and report a fire here at the Asylum."

"The Fire Department, Sir?" asked Worthington.

"Yes, exactly," Brent answered. "We can't trust the police."

Worthington pleaded with him. "Sir, are you certain about this? Even with your newfound... abilities, I'm rather concerned for your well being."

"Don't worry, Worthington," Brent assured him. "My legs are getting stronger every minute. I'll be fine. It's Miss Rose I'm most worried about."

"It's not your legs I'm most concerned about," Worthington responded.

Brent was silent for a long moment, then answered. "All those times I just wanted to cry, to give in... and you told me to be strong."

Brent reached up and clutched Worthington's shoulder like a son to a father. "Now I know why. Thank you, Worthington."

Moments later, Worthington watched as Brent emerged from the car. The cloak nearly engulfed him. Even without using his skill of disappearing, he blended easily with the night shadows that surrounded them. The only thing that could be seen was the glowing white skull of his mask. It was an unsettling sight indeed. He pulled his rosary from his pocket and clutched the beads tightly within his fingers.

Brent leaped quickly to the roof of the car, then with one swift move, he gracefully hurled himself straight over the fence. Not even the barbed wire slowed him down. Landing was another matter though, and Brent quickly lost his footing as soon as he touched the ground.

Worthington bolted from the car, clutching the iron fence, certain that Brent had already been injured.

Brent stood up, unharmed. "I think I'll need more practice on that. Don't forget. Twenty minutes."

Worthington nodded, "Do be careful, Sir."

He stood watching at the barricade as Master Gregor disappeared into the shadows of the asylum grounds. In all the years that he had cared for his employer, he'd never had to worry much for him. Not in many, many years anyway. As those thoughts came drifting back into his mind, he dutifully went back to the car.

Brent kept to the shadows and with some difficulty, headed up the side yard. The landing had been harder on him than he'd let on, and he was still getting used to walking again. It had been a painful process and now the pain was already coming back. When he was sure that he was out of Worthington's sight, he stopped to rub his thigh muscles. He would have to ignore it and press on. Harder to ignore, though, were the many terrible memories of this place from his childhood.

Despite the pain, he felt the Spirit Force stirring inside him. Other memories of past lives flashed in his mind. Memories of battles fought and won. Of wrongs righted. Of justice having prevailed. But most of all, deep within, he felt that he was no longer Brent Gregor, "crippled son of the murdered D.A." or the "crippled boy with the crazy mother." No, now he was something else entirely. He was The Black Spectre, and he was on a mission once again. Deep in his mind, however, lurked the realization that the memories of victory were not truly his own. He had limited dominion over his newfound powers and he could barely walk. He hoped it would be enough.

As he reached the front of the building, there was no sign of Vicky's car. The Spectre disappeared into the shadows again to survey the main lawn. He hadn't been there in years, but every detail was just as he remembered it. The tall, solid front doors surrounded by a deep stone alcove. The dark bricks that stretched to the night sky on the tall, prison-like walls. The black iron gates that covered each window. Seeing this place again filled him with fear and painful childhood memories.

Just then, a car pulled to a stop at the front door. The Spectre watched curiously as a tall, gangly man strode with purpose towards the door. This could be his opportunity to get inside completely unseen.

The Black Spectre moved in behind him. Just as the tall man reached the door, he stopped short and turned back to the car. The Spectre managed to vanish just in time. The tall man stopped short again near the car and turned back to the door, staring at it nervously. The Spectre watched as he did this several times before finally steeling his courage to go inside. The Spectre slid in right behind him just as the door swung shut.

The inside was just as he remembered it, too. The deep wood of the nurses' desk surrounded by gleaming tile floors, the dark hallways that turned off in both directions, the smell of disinfectant that choked the air.

The tall man felt something brush past him and looked around. Seeing nothing, he shrugged and went to the Nurse stationed at the front desk. "May I help you?" She asked.

The Spectre watched from the shadows of the room as the tall man nervously introduced himself. "Good evening, I'm Denny Morris. I'm with the *Daily Crusader*." The Spectre quickly realized that this was Vicky's friend with whom he'd spoken on the phone.

"I'm trying to locate one of our reporters, Miss Vicky Rose. No one's seen her for several hours and I understand that she stopped by here earlier. Would you happen to have seen her?" Denny asked, the worry in his voice very apparent.

"No," she answered, afraid to look him in the eye. "I'm afraid not. She hasn't been by here that I'm aware of, and I've been on duty since 2:00 this afternoon."

"Could anyone have seen her?" Denny implored, leaning over the desk. He wasn't entirely convinced that the Nurse was telling the truth. "I'm *certain* she was here."

"I can check with Dr. Hyneman. He would know for sure," she answered as she backed away, needing to defer to both a higher authority and a better liar. She pointed Denny to a small cluster of cushioned, high-back chairs near the door. "You can wait over there."

"Thank you," Denny replied, feeling a little more sure of himself as she picked up the phone.

The Spectre took the opportunity to make his way down the hallway. Denny thought he saw something move as he walked toward the chairs, but saw nothing when he looked again.

THE BLACK SPECTRE rounded the corner into an empty hallway with offices nearby. This was the path they'd always taken to visit his mother. She'd originally been on the second floor. He didn't want to follow this same path, but it was what he knew.

With the pain in his legs increasing, he needed to conserve his powers as much as possible. He commanded the light switch to turn off, rather than having to remain unseen. He checked the name on a nearby office door. "Dr. Emil Hyneman." He remembered the name from his conversation with Vicky. This was exactly what he wanted to find.

The door was locked, but that was no matter. The Spectre used the Spirit Force again and opened the door. Just as he closed it behind him, he heard the Front Desk Nurse page Dr. Hyneman. "Dr. Hyneman, please come to the front desk. You have a visitor."

CHAPTER TWENTY-ONE

DOWNSTAIRS in the basement lab, Dr. Hyneman was visibly irritated when he heard the page. He ordered Vito Spats to find out who it was.

Vicky welcomed any distraction, hoping this would take them away, that her prayers had been answered.

Dr. Hyneman quickly sensed her emotions. "Don't get too excited, my dear. No one can save you now," he told her with a smile.

Vito Spats went back out through the double doors.

THE SPECTRE looked around Dr. Hyneman's office. He knew this place, too. It had been Dr. Kobler's office years before. Dr. Kobler was always pleasant enough with Worthington, but seemed to hold little regard for young Brent. Getting his mind back into the present, he immediately found a purse sitting on the desk. It looked like Vicky's. He quickly scoured the contents and found her press pass inside. She had definitely been there.

He rushed back out into the darkened hallway, unsure of which way to go next. Upstairs or down? The last place he wanted to go was down.

WORTHINGTON sat still in the car, moving his fingers along the beads of his rosary and reciting silent prayers. The longer he sat and prayed, the more the distant, sad memories of one horrible night came rushing back to him. Try as he might, he couldn't get the thoughts out of his mind.

They became suddenly vivid, as if he were reliving them all over again. The sights and sounds filled his mind from when he rushed into Thomas Gregor's study and was taken aback by the most frightening sight.

The body of his employer, Thomas Gregor, lie face down on the desk in a pool of blood that dripped down the front. On the floor beneath his empty hand was a letter opener.

Beside the desk was Sarah Gregor, hysterical and crying.

But worst of all, there on the floor at his feet was young Master Gregor, bleeding from a bullet wound to his side. The child was turning grey and going into shock.

Worthington had to shake himself free of the vivid memories and bring himself back into focus on the task at hand.

He checked his watch. Less than ten minutes had passed.

He looked out the window at the imposing Asylum. All was quiet. Perhaps that was a good sign.

He hoped that it was.

DENNY sat waiting, fidgeting. He wondered what could be taking so long. It was late. The Asylum was closed. What could the Doctor possibly be doing at this hour, he wondered.

Sensing his impatience, the Nurse told him, "I'm waiting for Dr. Hyneman to call. It should only be a minute."

Practically on cue, the phone rang. The Nurse answered, but spoke in a voice too hushed for Denny to overhear. She nodded several times before hanging up.

Denny stood up when she looked in his direction, smiling pleasantly. "I'm sorry. I'm afraid Dr. Hyneman is unavailable right now, but you're welcome to come back to-morrow."

Denny pleaded, "Please, I need to see him right away."

The Nurse was firm. "I'm sorry, but you'll just have to come back to-morrow."

Dejected, Denny hung his shoulders low and went back to the door. As he reached for the knob, all he could think about was Vicky. Between the two of them, she was certainly the more courageous. Since he'd met her, she'd done things he'd only read about in dime novels. And now that Vicky needed him, he was turning into the coward he'd always been and just walking away.

Summoning courage that he didn't know he even had, Denny turned back and announced, "Look, I know she's here. So I'm just going to have to go find her myself."

"No, I can't let you do that, Sir," the Nurse protested, jumping up from her chair. But Denny marched right past her, rounding the same corner that The Spectre had taken just a short time before.

She darted back to her desk and breathlessly paged that a man was loose in the building.

CHAPTER TWENTY-TWO

ANGERED by yet another interruption, Dr. Hyneman barked to Vito Spats and Turkle to find this new intruder. "I can't have any more disruptions, or witnesses!"

Vito Spats jerked his pistol from his shoulder holster and said, "Don't worry about it."

Dr. Hyneman ordered Ned to stand outside the door. "Make sure no one gets in."

DENNY heard the page, too, and was instantly frustrated. He hadn't gotten very far at all. All he wanted to do was to find Vicky, and he couldn't even manage to do that. He wondered if maybe he should never have set foot in this place.

It only seemed like seconds later before he heard footsteps rushing down the hall towards him. Which way to go, he wondered. Without time to think, he ducked into the nearby stairwell and went upstairs to the second floor.

THE SPECTRE wasn't as lucky. Since he was no longer hiding in the shadows, the Orderlies summoned by Dr. Hyneman spotted him before he even knew they were approaching. Granted, he was still just a silhouette before them in the darkened hallway, but he had been spotted.

"You there! Stop!" one of them shouted.

The two large Orderlies, used to wrestling with the insane, raced down the dark hallway towards him. Stuck in a dead end with no means of escape, The Spectre was forced to defend himself. He needn't have worried. Instinct and distant memories immediately took over. He moved without even thinking. His only fear was whether or not his body was up to the task.

He decked the first Orderly with a solid punch to the face, knocking him off balance. With a swift kick and a turn, he pinned the dazed man against the wall with a boot to the neck. Then let him drop to the floor, choking for air.

With lightning speed, The Spectre grabbed the second Orderly from behind and forced him to the floor with his arm twisted in a firm lock.

"Tell me where Miss Rose is!" The Black Spectre demanded.

The Orderly struggled against the dark figure's iron grip, his other arm flailing. There was no escape for him.

"Where is she?" The Spectre shouted, giving the Orderly's arm a quick jerk that cleanly snapped the bone. The defeated man gave a short whimper before answering.

"She's down in the lab!" he pleaded. "In the basement!"

The Spectre stood silently for a moment, the second Orderly still firmly in his grip, the first still gasping for breath. The last place he wanted to go was downstairs. But he had no choice. He let the Orderlies go and dashed off for the stairwell.

DENNY searched through room after room, trying desperately to find Vicky. Every doorway held one disturbing surprise after another — patients kept behind locked doors, strapped to their beds, and crying out to him for help.

This "rescue" had turned into a nightmare. He was now convinced that he was no man for the job. He needed help, but knew there was none to be found.

Scared but determined, Denny continued his search.

WORTHINGTON checked his watch. Eight minutes to go.

He gripped his rosary tightly to his chest. Were it not for his faith, fear would have surely decimated him.

Try as he might, he just couldn't keep those terrible memories from invading his mind. He hadn't thought of it in years, but now that Master Gregor could be facing death again, the thoughts came racing back despite his best efforts.

Worthington remembered how he barely had time to react to the situation before Nanny Miriam and two of the maids, Agnes and Sally, rushed in behind him. All three women erupted into screams as soon as they saw the carnage through the doorway.

Worthington had no choice but to put his own emotions aside and take control. Quickly, he asked God for strength then commanded the women to compose themselves.

He rushed in the study and pulled Sarah Gregor to her feet. Holding her tightly, clutching her to his chest to shield her eyes, he rushed her out of the room and into the waiting arms of the maids. Then he ordered Nanny Miriam to call the police, an ambulance, and Dr. Wellman, who lived just a few blocks away. "Hurry!"

Dutifully, the women did just as he instructed. Then he turned back to the room. Thomas Gregor was clearly dead, so there was no use checking on him. He went straight to Master Brent who lay in a pool of his own blood, life quickly draining from his young body. He prayed again that it was not too late to save the boy.

Bringing himself back into focus again, he looked out the car window at the distant building.

Lights were now on in both the second and third floors.

This did not look good.

CHAPTER TWENTY-THREE

DR. HYNEMAN looked up proudly from his instruments and smiled wickedly with a demented look in his eye. "We're just about ready, my dear," he told Vicky. She didn't share in his enthusiasm. "The equipment is fully powered up," he added gleefully. "I just have to do a quick *test*."

Vicky watched in terror as he grasped two electronic prongs with enormous power cords running to the equipment.

"Get Turkle over here," Dr. Hyneman ordered.

Before Turkle could register what was going on, Ned and Vito Spats scooped him up beneath the arms and drug him over to Dr. Hyneman. "Wait a minute, Doc!" pleaded Turkle.

"Strap him into the chair," Dr. Hyneman commanded further.

"Doc, please," begged Turkle, "Come on! You can't do this to me! I done everything you ever told me!"

"Not quite," Dr. Hyneman answered with a leer of disgust. "You were supposed to run Miss Rose's car off the road, teach her a lesson, see that she learned to back off. According to my contacts in the police department, she easily outran you. Not very intimidating, if you ask me. Or Big Jack."

Turkle swallowed hard. He didn't want to think what was in store for him.

Dr. Hyneman then looked straight at Vicky and said with a malicious grin, "Don't worry Turkle, this will only hurt a lot."

Turkle tried to break loose from Vito Spat's iron grip, but found his efforts futile. Vito Spats and Ned strapped Turkle into a straight jacket and plopped him securely into the waiting chair.

Vicky couldn't believe her eyes as she watched Dr. Hyneman gleefully descend upon his waiting victim. It was all the more frightening just knowing that she was next.

"Put the stick in his mouth," Dr. Hyneman ordered. "He'll need it."

Ned picked up a short, wooden dowel that was already riddled with bite marks and jammed it between Turkle's teeth. Turkle pleaded wide-eyed as Dr. Hyneman touched the prongs to specific areas of his head, sending quick jolts of electricity into his cranium. Turkle's screams were barely muffled as he bit down ferociously on the dowel. The lights in the building dimmed on and off as the surges coursed through Turkle's body.

WORTHINGTON saw all the lights in the building flicker from outside. It was a disconcerting sight.

Was Master Gregor safe? He had no way to know.

No matter how hard he tried, he couldn't keep himself from thinking about that night. How it haunted him!

Bending down to the young Master, tears welled up in his eyes. As much as he wanted to break down himself, duty came first. Tears would come later.

Quickly removing his outer shirt, he used it to curtail the bleeding. He carefully lifted the shaking boy into his arms and held him until Dr. Wellman arrived.

Stroking the boy's hair, Worthington told him not to worry. "You're going to be just fine, my boy. Don't be afraid. You're going to be just fine."

Snapping back to the present again, he was worried more than ever. He started the car and put it into gear.

Just as he was about to speed off, he looked at his watch once more. "Master Gregor said twenty minutes. No matter what."

He obediently turned off the car and waited.

Duty came first.

"Dear God, please watch over him."

THE BLACK SPECTRE watched as the lights flickered in the stairwell and snapped him back into the present. He'd stopped at the stairwell door, crippled by his memories of the Asylum. The last time he'd been there he swore that he'd never return. He'd seen something there that he never wanted to see. A memory he had since tried over and over to erase from his mind.

It was there, in the basement level, just a few years previous, where his Mother had spent her last days. It was also there that Brent, then a young man in college, saw her for the last time, just a few months before she died. He had been home for the summer, his last before Senior year. After the violent outburst from their previous visit together, he'd promised Abbie never to see her again. And with very good reason.

But Brent felt guilty about making such a promise. They didn't know how much longer she would last. She'd called for him almost every day. He felt it was his duty as a son to see his mother.

Worthington had pushed him in his wheelchair as Dr. Kobler led them to the elevator and pressed the Down button.

"Why are we going downstairs?" Brent asked. "Mother's room is on the top floor."

Dr. Kobler turned and answered with the same disdainful look that he'd given Brent many times before. Since he was grown by then, he disliked that look even more. "Your mother is not well. We've had to remove her from the general population."

Brent looked to Worthington for answers, but only received the same stoic reserve he'd always displayed. The three of them were silent as they rode the elevator down and Dr. Kobler led them through the dark, snaking hallways of the basement level. Brent was barely able to fathom that his mother could end up in such a place.

When at last they reached his mother's room, Dr. Kobler opened the door.

"Be strong, Master Gregor," was all Worthington said as Dr. Kobler wheeled Brent inside.

Brent looked in shock as his mother stared back at him,

her eyes filled with something he would never be able to describe. Sarah Gregor was no longer the loving, beautiful woman that had cared for him as a child. She was no longer even the distant and vacant woman that she'd been for the last many years. No, hers had become the face of sheer madness and her insane screams pierced Brent to the core of his very being.

Thankfully, it was the flickering lights in the stairwell that finally brought him out of those memories and reminded him of why he was there.

DR. HYNEMAN continued the process in two more places on Turkle's skull. By the time he was finished, Turkle slumped over in the chair. Vicky watched in wide-eyed fear as the dowel fell out of his mouth and rolled on the floor to a stop by her gurney.

"Get him out of the jacket and give him the smelling salts," ordered Dr. Hyneman. "And don't let him see the jacket or our lovely Miss Rose here."

Dr. Hyneman turned Turkle's chair so that his back was towards Vicky and he was facing the doorway out. After several waves of smelling salts beneath his nose, Turkle finally coughed his way to consciousness.

Vicky watched as Dr. Hyneman put away the prongs and kneeled down to face Turkle.

"Turkle, listen to me," he beckoned, smiling triumphantly.

Turkle blinked his eyes and looked up groggily, drooling. "What happened, Doc?"

"How do you feel?" Dr. Hyneman asked.

"My head..." Turkle mumbled. "It's killing me." Dr. Hyneman gave Vito Spats a satisfied look.

"Turkle, I need to ask you something," Dr. Hyneman continued. "Tell me, has that girl reporter been here to-day?"

"No, Doc," Turkle answered.

"Are you sure?" Dr. Hyneman asked.

"Huh?" Turkle asked, barely able to stay focused.

"Very good," said Dr. Hyneman. "Why don't you go back to your room and rest for a while?"

"Thanks, Doc," said Turkle, rubbing his head. Turkle

tried to stand and immediately slumped to the floor.

Dr. Hyneman called for the remaining two Orderlies that stood guard outside the laboratory doors.

"Why don't you two help Mr. Turkle back to his room, will you?" he asked.

"Yes, of course, Doctor," they responded as they scooped Turkle up under the arms and lead him out of the lab.

"I'm putting it on a higher setting for Miss Rose," Dr. Hyneman told Ned and Vito Spats. "Everything she has known for the past few months will be wiped perfectly clean from her memory. If she survives, of course."

Vicky screamed again to no avail.

CHAPTER TWENTY-FOUR

THE BLACK SPECTRE stepped out of the stairway door, into the pitch dark basement level hallway. He was immediately struck by the unfamiliarity of it all. It wasn't just the darkness. This was another section of the lowest level, some distance away from the elevator where he'd been before.

As he rounded the corner, he found three more Orderlies heading straight towards him. If he kept to the shadows, he could conserve his powers and let them pass.

Such luck was not with him, however. Just as the Orderlies reached him, the lights came back on. The Spectre suddenly found himself face-to-face with the large, burly men.

"There he is!" One of them shouted. They rushed on him instantly.

Without time to think, The Spectre sprang on them like a loosened coil. He leaped off the wall and over their heads, landed right behind them and took down two with a sweeping kick across the floor beneath their feet. The two men collapsed like a sack of potatoes. The sounds of their bodies hitting the floor and the loud grunts that followed echoed down the hall.

The third Orderly swung back around and immediately adopted a stance that showed him to be a former boxer. He charged straight at The Spectre and with fists flying in quick, deliberate jabs.

Blow after blow only met with empty air, however, as The

Spectre easily dodged his punches. Making his move, The Spectre went in with a hard kick to the gut, then another to the head that took the man straight down.

The other two Orderlies struggled back to their feet, attempted to shake off their dazed conditions, and went after him again. The Spectre grabbed the first one in a headlock and used him to shield the punches of the other. He then knocked the attacking Orderly out with a swift kick to the head. A quick blow with his elbow took out the one still in his grip.

With his opponents subdued by pain, The Spectre crumbled to the floor. The fight had taken a lot out of him and the pain in his legs was getting worse. He could barely walk now, and if he didn't find Vicky soon, he wasn't sure if he'd be able to get himself out of there, much less her as well.

The Spectre checked his watch.

Just two more minutes.

DENNY found himself surrounded by four Orderlies in the hallway. He was no match for even one of them. His only option was to run and run fast, but these were men used to chasing patients. They easily caught up with him and wrestled him to the floor.

"Let me go!" he shouted.

Chuckling at his useless struggles, three of them drug him to the elevator. One Orderly told the remaining fourth, "Call Vito Spats. Tell him we've got his man. Meet us downstairs."

Once inside the elevator, an Orderly pushed the button for the basement level.

THE SPECTRE peered around the corner of an empty hallway. As soon as he saw the elevator, he knew exactly where he was. It had only been a few short years since he had been there last. But as he had guessed, he was some distance from where he'd entered via the stairwell.

Just then, the elevator bell sounded. Someone was coming.

He barely had time to register the thought before the

doors opened. He immediately ducked into the shadows, no longer able to hide completely. He was startled to see three Orderlies drag Denny out of the elevator and down the hall.

Staying far enough back to remain silent and unseen without the use of his powers, The Spectre followed them down the hall where they disappeared around the next corner and deeper into the bowels of the Asylum.

The Spectre kept pace behind them and looked around the final corner just in time to see the Orderlies haul Denny through a pair of double doors, past a large man standing guard.

The Spectre recognized this man. He knew that face. He knew the shape of his form. He especially knew the hand with only three fingers. Though age had changed the image from what had been etched in his memory forever, it was still unmistakable.

He'd never forget "Three-Finger Ned" Vogel.

He'd never forget the night that Ned shot him.

He'd never forget the pain he'd felt when the bullet entered his young flesh.

Or the horror of seeing his mother fall.

Or the anguish of seeing his father murdered.

There was only one thing worse than having to return to this place and relive the final, searing memory of his mother.

And this was it.

CHAPTER TWENTY-FIVE

VITO SPATS and Dr. Hyneman looked up at the Orderlies as they shoved Denny into the lab.

"Finally!" Dr. Hyneman shouted. "Keep him subdued!"

"Denny!" Vicky shouted through her gag.

"You let her go!" Denny shouted, struggling against his captors. By some stroke of luck, Denny proved himself more slippery than they expected and managed to slip free from their grip. He rushed straight to Vicky's side.

He didn't get far, though.

Vito Spats pistol whipped him on the back of the head.

Vicky screamed through her gag as Denny slumped to the cold tile floor like a rag doll. Vito kicked him over to get a look at this face.

"Who is this guy?" Vito asked, looking at Vicky. "This your boyfriend, Sweetheart? Coming to your rescue, eh?"

The Orderlies shrugged. Dr. Hyneman answered, "I believe he works for the same newspaper."

Vito took Denny's wallet and searched through it. "He don't got a press pass. Can't be too important. I don't care what you say, Doc. I'm taking this one for a ride."

Tears rolled down Vicky's face. This had gotten far worse than before.

WORTHINGTON watched impatiently as the second hand on his watch completed its final rotation.

He fought the memories of holding young Brent in his arms and how the boy's blood gradually soaked the crisp sleeves of his starched white shirt. How he clutched the boy tightly and watched his skin grow ever more pale as the very life ran from his small form. How he prayed over and over that God would see fit to save the boy and keep him on this earth.

He remembered the sudden relief he felt when Dr. Wellman rushed in, wearing a robe over his dress pants, and ordered him to carry young Brent to the kitchen. How he did just as the Doctor commanded him and gently lay Brent on the kitchen table as Wellman hurriedly retrieved tape and gauze from his bag to stop the bleeding.

He remembered Dr. Wellman placing a comforting, blood-stained hand on his shoulder. The Doctor told him not to worry, that the ambulance would be there soon. Dr. Wellman felt sure that the boy would live.

He remembered falling on his knees in prayer right there in the kitchen, thanking God for His infinite mercy.

Those last few seconds seemed to take an eternity.

Finally, twenty minutes had passed. To the second.

Now it was time to act. To fulfill his duty.

Worthington started the car again and sped off. Not willing to lose one second more.

THE SPECTRE stared down the hall at the lone figure that stood between him and reaching Vicky and Denny. Try as he might, he couldn't get past the fears that had haunted him these past fifteen years. The memories came rushing back.

The Spectre — no, Brent Gregor — saw his beautiful mother, Sarah, drop to the floor as Ned whipped around to face him. The gun rang out in the same instant that Ned's eyes locked with his. He could hear his parents scream. He could see Ned's expression change momentarily when he realized that Brent was just a kid, too late to stop the bullet that was rushing towards him. A bullet that ripped into his side and knocked him to the floor.

Brent saw his father, Thomas, rush towards Ned, the sharp letter opener in his hand. His father lunged at Ned, going for his throat, ready to kill in order to defend his wife and son. He saw the second shot ring out, the one that hit his father directly in the chest. He saw his father fall once again, dropping face first onto the desk.

His legs giving out, Brent crumbled to the floor, crying. He was no longer silent. No longer unseen.

"Who's there?" Ned called out.

CHAPTER TWENTY-SIX

VICKY watched helplessly as Vito Spats tried to fasten Denny into the straight jacket. "Don't you got any rope?" he asked.

Frustrated, Dr. Hyneman said, "No! We don't use such barbaric means here." He shouted to the Orderlies, "Help him out, will you! I've had enough of these interruptions!"

"Don't worry, Doc," Vito Spats told him. "You won't be having any trouble from this one no more."

NED called out again. "Who's there?"

Clenching his fists and fighting back both the pain in his legs and his soul, The Black Spectre summoned what remained of his strength. He stepped quietly from the shadows, visible only as a dark silhouette in the dim hallway.

"Who are you?" Ned asked.

"A ghost from your past," answered The Spectre, his anger building up within him. "I've come for revenge."

Ned chuckled. "Oh, yeah? Well, let's just see about that."

The Spectre moved on him in a flash, striking several blows with such speed and grace that the large, hulking man was unable to defend himself.

Ned stumbled, but he didn't go down. He could take a punch, and he'd been dealt worse.

As soon as The Spectre backed off from his attack, Ned made his move. He swung low and he swung hard.

Despite his newfound skills and abilities, The Spectre

wasn't prepared for it. He saw it coming, and had the split-second realization that he couldn't block it, nor could he duck.

Ned's fist hammered directly into his chest. The crushing blow sent him sprawling across the hallway floor.

WORTHINGTON sped to a halt at the nearest phone booth, jumping out of the car. He stopped short when he saw that it was already taken.

Worthington waited impatiently, only for a few seconds, before banging on the door.

"Please, Sir! This is an emergency."

The Man in the booth looked back at him, disgruntled, "What, you late for cocktail hour?"

NED peered into the darkness to get a better look at his opponent. All he could see was a dark figure draped in a cloak that hid the extent of his form. The only detail he could truly make out was the gleaming white skull that stared back at him.

For a moment, Ned felt a shiver of his own. He wondered if he were facing Death himself. But no matter if this were the Grim Reaper or not, Ned wasn't about to go down without a fight.

The Spectre struggled back to his feet, clutching the pain in his chest that now battled for dominance over the pain in his legs. All that was blocked from his mind, however, when he looked up at Ned's grimacing face. The only thing he could see in his mind at that moment was the memory of that bullet tearing into him. Over and over, he saw it again, unable to clear that instant from his thoughts.

His legs were weak. His chest was pounding. His powers were nearly drained. Clearly, he wasn't ready to face Ned again.

Perhaps he never would be.

He tried to make his next move, but it was too late. Ned slugged him hard and sent him sprawling once more.

Trying to clear his head, The Spectre did his best to crawl away. Escape was his only remaining option. And even that seemed impossible now.

Ned grabbed his cloak and drug him back, laughing. "You ain't getting away from me, Ghost Man!"

Ned held him up to eye-level, shouting, "You ain't no devil!" and decked him once more.

This time The Spectre hit the wall before collapsing into the shadows.

If he couldn't walk, The Spectre reasoned, perhaps there were enough of his powers left to hide. Summoning all that he had left, he vanished from sight.

Ned stormed down the hall, looking for him.

"Where are you?" Ned demanded. "Come back here, you lily-livered coward! I ain't scared of you! I ain't scared of nothing!"

If he were going to escape from Ned, The Spectre would have to think smarter.

Twenty minutes were well past. The Fire Department should be there soon.

It seemed his only option for survival.

CHAPTER TWENTY-SEVEN

WORTHINGTON knocked impatiently on the phone booth again. "Please, Sir," he begged. "This is a life-or-death emergency! I must call the Fire Department!"

The Man didn't even look back when he told him, "Buzz off, will you?"

In his younger years, Worthington could have pulled the inconsiderate Man from the booth and flattened him, but at his age, he was no match and time was growing short.

Worthington looked around. Perhaps there was another phone booth nearby. There was a bar across the street.

Worthington raced inside and found an empty phone booth in the back. Quickly, he called the Fire Department and dutifully reported a fire at the Asylum.

THE SPECTRE scurried deeper into the shadows in a desperate attempt to hide from Ned, but his draining powers and the pain in his legs kept him from staying hidden. Ned stormed the hallway like a bloodhound sniffing a trail, and it was only moments before he found The Spectre cowering in a dark corner.

Ned grabbed him by the cloak again and drug him back down the hall. "You ain't getting away from me!" Ned laughed as he flung him spinning across the slick, tiled floor.

The Spectre tried to scurry away again. If only he could escape Ned long enough to clear his mind and gather his strength. But it was not to be. Ned's thundering foot stomped down on his cloak, bringing him to a sudden stop like a frightened dog that's reached the end of its leash.

Ned reached down and grabbed The Spectre's cloak in his large, sinewy hands. Hand over hand, he tugged the cloak until he finally had The Spectre by the collar. He hoisted the Spectre's limp figure up to his chest, finally getting a good look at his opponent's skull mask.

"What are you supposed to be, anyway?" Ned asked, chuckling as he waited for an answer. The Spectre was silent.

Ned hoisted him up to eye level, then said, "Boo!"

VICKY cried with widened eyes again as Dr. Hyneman loomed over her, prongs in hand, ready to apply the electricity to wipe the memories from her mind. "Finally, everything is ready!" he proclaimed.

She let out a final, pleading scream, barely muffled by the leather gag, as Dr. Hyneman put the prongs to her head and the first jolts coursed through her skull. She was only conscious for a moment longer, blacking out just as The Black Spectre was thrown through the double doors and slid across the floor like a rag doll thrown by an angry child.

Dr. Hyneman jumped back, startled and fuming. He'd barely gotten started. "What the devil —!" he shrieked.

Ned burst through the doors right behind The Spectre. "Doc! We got us another intruder!"

Vito Spats aimed his pistol at the moaning, dark-cloaked figure on the floor.

"Was there an open invitation to come to the Asylum to-night?" asked Dr. Hyneman.

"Probably looking for the Broad, too," Vito Spats added. "I told you, we should just get rid of her."

Like the others, he was rather puzzled by The Spectre's appearance. "What's this guy dressed up for, Halloween?"

"Just see to it that he remains subdued," Dr. Hyneman ordered Ned.

"Don't worry, Doc," Ned assured him. "This guy ain't nothing."

Brent looked up and saw the master power switch on

the wall. Concentrating with all his might, he focused his remaining powers on the switch. It struggled in its cradle. Closing his eyes and focusing more, the switch finally broke free and slammed all the way down. The room was bathed in almost total darkness. Vito Spats and Ned both felt a chill in the air.

"There's a spirit in here," Vito Spats said, looking around nervously. It was too dark to see anything.

"Nonsense," said Dr. Hyneman, feeling his way across the room to the switch. He turned the lights back on.

"See?" asked Hyneman. "It was just the power switch."

Instinctively, Vito Spats and Ned both looked to where The Spectre had been lying on the floor.

He was gone.

"Then what happened to the Ghost Man?" Ned asked.

Just then, the lights shut off again.

"What the devil?" Hyneman asked, reaching back for the switch. Just as he grabbed it, a book sailed from out of nowhere and hit him square in the head. "Who threw that?"

"I swear, it won't me!" shouted Ned, just as he was pummeled by three more books that were hurtled through the darkness.

Vito Spats aimed his gun in various directions, completely unsure of which way to face their attacker.

Ned looked around and was hit by a beaker that instantly shattered and drenched him in a foul-smelling liquid. "I'm getting out of here!" he shouted. He rushed to the back door, but found it locked.

"Get back here you frightened idiot!" Dr. Hyneman shouted.

Ned ignored him and raced out the double doors to the hallway. The Orderlies were right on his heels.

"Cowards!" shouted Dr. Hyneman.

Vito Spats scanned the darkness and fired at anything that looked like it might be moving.

Worried for his equipment, Dr. Hyneman rushed over to it. Just as he reached the cruel machine, the cords wrapped themselves around his neck like a pair of serpents. Dr. Hyneman struggled to get free, but they only tightened their grip even more. The prongs moved themselves to his forehead. "No, not that!" As Dr. Hyneman cried out, the lights came back on and he was jolted into silence. When the lights went out again, his crumpled, hissing form fell to the floor.

Vito Spats watched all this, dumbfounded. Nothing much scared him, but this was unlike anything he'd ever seen. He called out to the darkness. "I don't know who you are, but you ain't taking me down!" He reached for Vicky, but the gurney rolled away on its own.

Outside, the sound of approaching sirens filled the air. Vito knew that sound well enough, and knew it was time to leave. He cautiously backed towards the rear doors, his pistol ready, and threw one open. Taking a quick glance to make sure it was safe, he barreled up the deep, cement stairwell that lead up to the rear grounds of the estate. Within moments, he had disappeared into the darkness.

The Spectre cursed himself for having to let both Ned and Vito Spats get away, but he had been unprepared to face either.

He would face both men again on other days.

CHAPTER TWENTY-EIGHT

HAVING parked the car behind the Asylum again, Worthington watched a dark shadow run across the back lawn as the approaching sirens grew louder and louder. He wondered for a moment if it might be Master Gregor, but the build was wrong.

At the front of the building, he saw the fire trucks round a nearby corner and speed to a stop outside the ominous old building.

The Front Desk Nurse rushed out to the Firemen in a panic. "Please! There's an intruder loose in the Asylum!"

The Fire Chief looked at her, puzzled. "But where's the fire?"

"I don't know about any fire," she said. "But there's somebody running loose in there. The lights kept going on and off, and then I heard gunshots from down in the basement!"

"Don't worry, Ma'am," the Fire Chief told her. "We'll go check it out."

Worthington watched as the Chief led his men into the building. He prayed that Master Gregor and Miss Rose were safe.

BOTH Vicky and Denny were still unconscious. Denny was crumpled on the floor in his straight jacket and easy to reach. The Spectre crawled over and freed him easily enough, but Vicky was another matter. He grabbed the edge of the gurney then struggled to pull himself to where he could reach her as well. He quickly loosened Vicky from the straps.

"Miss Rose," he asked her, "are you all right?"

She moaned groggily, starting to awaken. She could barely make out the dark form that stood over her. Her vision had not yet recovered from the treatment and all that she could make out was the shape of a man.

"Who...?" was all she managed to ask.

Denny also started to come to.

Seeing that they both seemed well enough, The Spectre slumped back down to the floor and disappeared into the shadows once again.

Denny shook his head and then realized where he was. He looked up and saw Vicky on the gurney. He quickly crawled to his feet to find her rubbing her head. He clutched her tightly, asking, "Vicky, Vicky? Are you okay?"

She sat up, looking around with confusion. "I think so. My head is splitting, though. What happened?"

Denny pointed to Dr. Hyneman lying on the floor. "He did something to you. Something with that machine."

"He wanted to erase my memory," Vicky answered. "But that man stopped him."

"What man?" Denny asked.

"He was right here," Vicky explained. "Just a minute ago. He was all in black. He rescued me."

"I didn't see anyone else here," Denny stated. "Are you sure?"

"I thought I was," Vicky answered as she surveyed the room.

Just as Denny said, there was no sign of anyone else.

Perhaps it had just been her imagination. No one could have rescued her except for Denny, she realized.

The Firemen rushed in through the double doors and found Denny as he helped Vicky off the gurney. Denny was elated. From that and their disheveled appearance, it was clear that they were the victims of whatever scenario had occurred there.

"Chief, thank goodness you're here!" Denny shouted. "She needs help."

The Chief ordered his men to attend to Vicky, while he

went over to check Dr. Hyneman. "He's alive. Looks like he took quite a jolt, though, judging from the burn marks on his scalp."

"Chief," Denny explained, "that man kidnapped Miss Rose here and attempted to brainwash her using that machine. Then somehow, I don't know, he got shocked by it himself."

"Well," said the Chief, scratching his head, "probably best if we just get you all down to the police station and let them sort this whole mess out. Then maybe you can tell us who it was that called in a false alarm."

As the Chief got another of his men to help him put Dr. Hyneman on the gurney, the evil psychiatrist regained consciousness, but clearly not his senses.

"Where?" he asked, clearly confused.

The Chief answered as they wheeled him out, "The Asylum."

Dr. Hyneman had a sudden look of panic. "What?"

THE SIRENS and flashing lights of the fire trucks outside the asylum attracted a crowd like moths to a flame. Soon a huge swarm of onlookers had invaded the normally closed-off asylum grounds and gathered outside the front doors. Questions with no answers filled the air.

"What's going on?" the gawkers asked of each other.

"Is it a fire? I don't see any smoke!"

"I heard somebody escaped."

"I heard somebody broke in."

Charlie Hecht and Ben Gelbart arrived to the cacophony and pushed their way through the hordes to get the inside scoop. They'd shove their way inside if they had to, and bribe any firemen necessary to get the story.

"Press!" Hecht shouted and held his notebook up as if it were a free pass to the front of the line. "Let us through!"

"Hey, watch it, Bub!" Someone shouted. "You hit me with your smoke!"

With a great deal of effort, they finally made it to the fire trucks and managed to corner a Young Fireman who sat on the end of a truck without his helmet or coat. Clearly to Hecht, this didn't look like much of a fire. He pulled a pencil from his pocket and made with the introduction.

"Charlie Hecht, *Terminal City Standard*. What's going on here?"

"We think it's a false alarm," the Young Fireman answered. "Chief went in a few minutes ago. We don't know what's going on. Heard maybe one of the inmates got out."

Gelbart scratched his head and dropped ashes in his hair, then quickly brushed them out. "Sounds pretty queer. We better go inside."

"Hey," Hecht asked the Young Fireman, "you see any other reporters around here?"

"No," the young fellow answered, "just you two."

Certain they had yet another scoop, Hecht thanked the fellow and forged back through the crowd to the front doors. His shouts of "Press! Press! Coming through!" only managed to clear a partial path before they finally made it to the Asylum entrance.

Gelbart looked up to see the Chief emerge. And right behind him were Vicky and Denny. She smiled at them.

"Hello, Boys!" she smiled triumphantly. "Looks like I beat you to it! Told you there was a story here."

"Story?" Gelbart panicked, "what story?"

Vicky leaned closer and Gelbart moved his cigarette out of her reach.

"You can read about it to-morrow in the *Crusader*," she told him, "Same as everyone else."

EPILOGUE

"EXTRA! EXTRA! Read all about it! O'Donnell innocent! Asylum Doctor Crazy! Three-Finger Ned still at large! Read all about it! Get your paper!"

The Newsboys shouted the headlines from virtually every street corner in Terminal City, selling papers with all the sordid details on what had happened at the Asylum (at least most of them), and how, thanks to Vicky Rose, Harvey O'Donnell had been freed from prison.

Once again, Frank edited out the best parts of Vicky's story. Once again, he didn't want to upset the Mob, so Vito Spats' involvement wasn't mentioned in the version that was printed. Once again, Vito Spats got off scot-free.

It didn't bother her this time, though. As she stood outside the prison with the other crime reporters, she took deep satisfaction in finally achieving her journalistic ambition. But that was nothing compared to the even deeper satisfaction she felt knowing that she was about to watch Harvey O'Donnell walk out as a free man. Justice had prevailed for once in Terminal City. It didn't happen often, but it was sure sweet when it did.

She was too elated to even mind when Hecht and Gelbart pushed their way over for yet another beef.

"So," Hecht jumped right in, "you think you're something, eh, Doll Face?"

Vicky just stood there and let him steam.

"Let me tell you something," Hecht ranted on, "don't think we're going to cut you any slack just because you're a skirt. I told you before. The newspaper game is no place for a dame, got it? It's a tough business. You just got lucky, that's all."

Gelbart blew smoke in her face for good measure.

Vicky just smiled back sweetly.

"I've been threatened by guys a lot tougher than you. See you on the street, Boys." She pushed her way past them and let her heels clack extra loud against the pavement for good measure.

Moments later, the crowd erupted as O'Donnell was escorted out of the prison and through the gates. Tears ran down his face as he rushed out to kiss his wife and hug his two young sons.

As O'Donnell was bombarded with questions from Hecht, Gelbart, and the gaggle of other reporters, Vicky just stood back and watched. Any other day, and many after this one, she would have forced her way to the front of the pack. But this time, she was content to just stand and watch the smiles on the O'Donnell's faces. Then she watched curiously as O'Donnell scanned the crowd to look for someone. Wondering who it could be, Vicky began to look herself. Vito Spats maybe? Someone to intimidate him, to warn him to stay quiet, especially now that he was a free man?

Vicky got her answer when O'Donnell's eyes locked on her own. He pushed through the reporters and gathered throng until he finally reached her. "Miss Rose, I read all your stories. And I just wanted to thank you. You're a braver man -- I mean, woman — I mean... you're a heck of a lot braver than I am, and I just wanted to thank you for it. If there's anything I can ever do to repay you, you just let me know."

Vicky was speechless, but her blushing and tears said all that was needed. Mrs. O'Donnell gave her a hug, and the boys both kissed her on the cheek. Hecht and Gelbart could only stand there and shake their heads.

Sometimes it helps to just try.

AFTER all the hoopla at the prison, Vicky was ready for a quiet night out with Denny.

As they sat at the table at Vicedomini's, Denny said, "Glad we finally got our dinner together."

"I am, too. This is just lovely. But, do you think we could stop by a soda fountain afterwards?"

Denny panicked. "It's too fancy, isn't it? I should tell you, though, the reason I picked this place is because my uncle is the Maitre d' and I knew he'd give us a good table."

"You mean you didn't bring me here to propose?" she teased.

"No, of course not," Denny blushed. "I mean, I'd love to, sure, but I don't think we're ready... what I'm trying to say is, I don't want to..."

"You just don't want to rush things," Vicky said.

"Right," answered Denny, relieved. "I would like to offer you a toast, though. To Vicky Rose, the most beautiful flower I know. To long life and good health."

She thanked him as they clicked their glasses.

As Vicky sipped her wine, she found her thoughts drifting off to someone else. The one person who'd provided the missing piece to the puzzle. The unsung hero who'd been all but forgotten in this whole sordid ordeal.

EARLY the next morning, Vicky went back to the Gregor Mansion. Worthington greeted her warmly, just as he would many times from that day forward, and led her to the library where she found Brent Gregor sitting in his wheelchair, a book in his blanket-covered lap as he stared out the window.

"Miss Rose, to what do I owe the honor?" he asked.

"I just wanted to thank you," she answered.

"For what?" he asked, curiously.

"For helping me solve this case," she told him. "If you hadn't helped, I may never have put it all together. Not only that, but if you hadn't told Denny where I was, Lord knows what would have happened to me."

"Well," Brent answered, "I didn't do much, but for my small part, I thank you for your appreciation. And I'm certainly glad that Mr. Morris was able to reach you in time."

Brent wheeled his chair closer to her. "I certainly enjoyed reading your depiction of the events. Made me feel like I was right there. And I also appreciate that you left me out of it. For that, I am very grateful. I especially like being an 'unnamed source'."

"I thought you would," she told him. "But if you don't mind my saying so, you don't always have to hide in this big old house. You can come out some time, you know." Vicky made her hint as obvious as possible, but he didn't seem to catch on.

"Yes," he replied, "perhaps."

After Vicky left, Brent stood at the window and watched her drive away. He remarked to Worthington, "She certainly is beautiful, isn't she, Worthington?"

"Yes, Sir," Worthington answered, "quite so. I believe she may find you somewhat appealing as well, Sir." Worthington thought for a moment. "You could have easily stood up and told her that you were the one who rescued her."

Brent shook his head. "Maybe, if she weren't a reporter. She certainly seems trustworthy, but she's still a reporter. No, I did my part last night. And I'm afraid that to keep on doing it, to pay the price I owe, Brent Gregor must forever stay bound to this wheelchair."

END.

If you enjoyed this book, please turn the page to read an excerpt of NO VICTORY WITHOUT SCARS, the next exciting chapter in the Black Spectre saga!

EXCERPT FROM
NO VICTORY WITHOUT SCARS (BOOK II)

CHAPTER ONE

OFFICER ROBERT SHAYNE sat by the third floor window of the Park Hotel on State Street. Tall, handsome, and clean-cut, a former military man who, in his dark blue uniform with shiny brass buttons, was the model of what a Terminal City police officer should be.

He took another drag from his cigarette as he watched the brick, two-story Quality Flour building across the street. From the outside it looked like a wholesome distributor. But anyone with any street smarts knew that this was where North Side Mob Boss Nails McCarthy ran his operations.

It was getting late in the afternoon and Shayne was ready for a break. He'd been staring out the window for hours, taking turns with three other flatfoots under the command of Detective Sergeant Michael Flynn.

Flynn was the near mirror opposite of Shayne. Dressed in a brown suit that looked a little too expensive for his weekly pay, he was thick around the middle and graying on top. A man who knew the city well and, thanks to his position, had found numerous ways to make it more comfortable.

Word on the street was that Whitey O'Leary was meeting up with Nails before skipping town. He'd been hiding out ever since gunning down two cops just a week earlier. They'd had the whole city on lockdown ever since. Whitey was a wanted man of the worst kind.

Shayne stubbed out his cigarette on the window sill. He really needed to stretch his legs for a minute.

Just as he was about to get up, he glanced out the window again and happened to spot a man round the corner. The fellow in question was cloaked in the afternoon shadows. And with a wide-brimmed hat on his head, it was difficult to see the man's face.

Shayne watched silently as the fellow looked casually about, making sure the coast was clear.

"Hey Boss," Shayne called to Flynn, "I think we got something here."

"Whitey?" Flynn asked, rushing to the window.

"Not yet," Shayne answered, straining for a better look. And wishing he'd brought a pair of binoculars. "I'm guessing that's Mossy Egan."

Since the Mob wars of the last few months, the North Side gang had lost a lot of ground. And major players. For that reason, a number of low-ranking hoods had all gotten promotions. Also, for that reason, the police weren't as familiar with all the new faces.

Flynn stepped up to the window, pinching his smoke tightly. Just standing there, watching, set his teeth on edge. He hoped this was their chance to get evens.

"Heh-lo," Shayne added as two more men rounded the corner and looked about with Mossy.

"That him?" Flynn asked, leaning over Shayne's shoulder for a closer look.

"Can't say for sure," Shayne answered, craning to study every detail of the two suspects. Without getting their attention or falling out of the window.

"The short one's got to be Kid Yellow Newman," Shayne asserted. He'd encountered him many times over while walking the beat.

Kid Yellow had a well-known penchant for picking pockets. And had the arrest record to prove it. Despite the tell-tale limp, he also had a reputation for hightailing it at the first sign of trouble. Hence the nickname.

"The other guy," he added, "I just don't know. I mean, it *looks* like Whitey, but I just can't say for sure."

Same height, same build. And best he could tell, same

hair color. Who else could it be?

They watched a moment longer as the two taller men ducked inside the building. Kid Yellow was left outside on watch. And was immediately distracted by a stray cat.

"That's gotta be him," Flynn stated emphatically. "Call down to the paddy wagon. Tell 'em were moving in."

Flynn stubbed out his own smoke on the sill and patted Shayne on the shoulder. "Good work, Bob. After to-day, you'll make Detective in no time."

DAILY CRUSADER reporter Vicky Rose was having an early dinner with her co-worker and new boyfriend, the lanky and studious Denny Morris. Denny worked in the paper's archives (affectionately known as "the morgue"), which fit his librarian-like personality.

For only their third date, Vicky had insisted on a booth at the nearby Cosmic Diner, which was all shiny surfaces and tile floors in its Art Deco interior. It wasn't that she had any affinity for the diner, other than it was very close to the office (so close that Frank usually stopped there for breakfast. And lunch). But primarily it was decidedly far-less romantic than the location of their first date, Vicedomini's, which was where couples usually went to propose.

Vicky knew full well (after Denny had defensively explained it), that the only reason he had chosen Vicedomini's was that his uncle was the Maitre'D. And for that reason he knew he could get a good table. And even a discount. All of which didn't make her insist on the Cosmic any less.

Either way, nothing could dampen the immense pride that Denny felt walking in with her on his arm.

It also didn't dampen Denny's efforts in constantly peppering her with questions regarding her family. Which unnerved her to no end. She wasn't about to introduce him to her father just yet. If ever.

Nor did her talking about an entirely different subject. "So you never saw the Man in Black?"

"No, I didn't," he answered in frustration.

Vicky just couldn't shake the topic from her mind. She

tried her best to recall, but the memories were too hazy. And considering who all was there, Denny was the only one with whom she felt comfortable discussing it.

"Well," she insisted for the umpteenth time, "someone asked me if I was okay and loosened the straps. You were still unconscious. You had to be."

Denny tried as he could to lay the issue to rest. At least as far as he was concerned. "I promise you. I never saw anyone else. But that's not what I was asking."

"Then what were you asking?" she replied in confusion.

"About your father," he reminded her.

"Look, Denny," she admonished, rubbing her temples, "I told you, I'm not interested in a full-blown courtship here. This is just for laughs right now, nothing more."

"I know, I know," he countered. "I'm just trying to get to know you a little better. What's the harm in that?"

It was his sweet-natured innocence that got to her. She knew he wanted something more from their relationship and would take it in a heartbeat. But if they were going to do this, he had to be understanding and take it slow.

"I already told you all about my family," she relented. "My mother's a teacher, and so's my sister. My brother works at the bank."

"What about your father?"

"The less said, the better," Vicky quickly retorted, rubbing her head again.

He'd noticed she'd been doing that quite a bit lately. Ever since that night at the Asylum.

"Do you think I use the word *puerile* too much?" she inquired, quickly changing the subject yet again.

"I don't know," he replied, puzzled. "Why?"

"Somebody mentioned it recently, that's all." She opened her eyes wide and put both hands to her head.

"Another migraine?" He couldn't help but be concerned. Even if she found his concern a little too forward. Just like everything else.

"It's nothing," she brushed him off. "Just a little headache. I'll be fine. 'Course, working under Lyons doesn't help."

Though she'd successfully made it to the crime beat, City Editor Frank Matson hadn't quite trusted her yet to work on her own. So he'd assigned her to shadow a senior reporter, Chester Lyons.

"So, you were saying about your father?" Denny queried gingerly, trying to coax her back towards the topic at hand.

"Like I told you before, we don't exactly get along anymore. He thinks being a reporter is unseemly."

She let out a brief sigh, then suddenly became more candid. "Had one foot in the grave for as long as I can remember. I'm always worried one day I'll get a call from my mother that something's happened. And then it'll be too late."

Denny was about to ask "too late for what?" But then he realized what she meant.

He struggled for something comforting to say, when suddenly it no longer mattered.

"Hey Vick," the Waiter shouted, interrupting. "Frank just called. The cops just raided Nails McCarthy's office up on the North Side."

"POLICE! It's a raid! Hands in the air!" Shayne shouted, pistol at the ready.

He stormed the lobby. Right behind him was a gun-wielding Flynn. Plus five more men in blue, all armed with shotguns.

The phone rang just as they barreled inside.

It was large room on the second floor. The walls were beige and mostly unadorned, save for a large Quality Flour sign. There was a small reception desk and a row of filing cabinets to the left. On the far right was a partially open office door. The top half had an opaque window that read "Manager."

To the casual observer, it looked just like any other respectable business.

The first clue to the contrary were four Irish toughs standing around the reception desk and having a smoke. They quickly put their hands up and all looked very surprised.

"Where's Whitey?" Flynn barked as the phone rang again.

No one answered.

The cops quickly surrounded the group and Shayne

frisked them for weapons. The two officers immediately recognized three of them as the men they'd seen down on the street. Kid Yellow, Mossy Egan, and... a fellow named Spike Kinney.

Who clearly wasn't Whitey O'Leary. But he sure looked like him from a distance.

The fourth ruffian was a red-headed bruiser named Cockeye Dunne. Who, of course, wasn't Whitey, either.

Damn.

Flynn rushed to the office door and was met by Dapper Sheridan, Nails' new right-hand man.

"Say, what's the idea?" Dapper snapped as the phone rang again behind him.

There was no mistaking him, either. With his bowler hat, three-piece suit, and finely trimmed moustache, he always looked like he'd just stepped out of the men's clothing pages of the Smithson & Gregor catalog.

"Where's Whitey?" Flynn demanded as he shoved his pistol into the young mobster's face.

"No idea," Dapper sputtered before Shayne grabbed him by the collar and shoved him toward the others.

"Get them out of here!" he commanded. "Arrest the lot of them!"

Inside the office, Jimmy "Nails" McCarthy stood beside a large, oak desk with his hands held high. His coat was on the chair and his suspenders the only thing over his shirt.

Shayne frisked him carefully as the phone rang one last time.

The office was just as plain as the lobby, except much smaller and with three open windows along the outside wall.

"Where's Whitey?" Flynn demanded again. He jabbed at Nails with his sidearm.

Nails just stood there — defiant.

That wasn't good enough. Shayne slugged Nails hard across the jaw. Then once more in the gut to make his point.

Nails doubled over for a second or two, but remained silent. Then he stood back up and looked Shayne straight in the eye. Defiant as ever. They didn't call him "Nails" for nothing.

"Don't make me ask you again," Flynn instructed. "There's a lot more where that come from."

Nails just stared back at him angrily. Then he finally responded through gritted teeth. "Don't know what you're talking about, Copper. Ain't seen him for weeks."

As Flynn paced angrily about, Shayne noticed that something on the desk had gotten Nails' attention.

"Don't toy with me, Jimmy," Flynn warned him angrily. "Word on the street is Whitey's been holding up and is meeting you here to-night. So you tell me! Where is that cop-killing bastard?"

Nails stayed silent.

Flynn slugged Nails himself just for good measure.

As Flynn turned around, Nails quickly grabbed a scrap of paper from the desk and shoved it in his mouth.

"He's trying to swallow something!" Shayne alerted. He quickly grabbed Nails by the jaw, but the Irish ganglord held tough and refused to spit it out.

Shayne drove three solid punches straight into his gut. Nails coughed and gagged, but still refused.

Flynn hit his breaking point. "You think you're tough, do ya?" he shouted in Nails' ear.

He pressed his pistol against the right side of Nails' chest and pulled the trigger.

As Nails winced in horrible pain, he finally spun around and opened his mouth. The paper fell out onto the floor.

Then Flynn shot him twice more. First in the neck, and again in the back.

Nails finally crumbled to the floor, screaming in agony.

"Ain't so tough now, are you boy?" Flynn shouted angrily.

Shayne just stood there in stunned silence.

"Pick that up, will ya?" Flynn asked as he shrugged in resignation. Then he raised his pistol to his own arm and pulled the trigger.

The round just barely grazed him. But it was enough to rip through his jacket and cause him to bleed.

Moments later, Flynn stormed out of the building, clutching his injured arm.

"I been shot!" he cried out.

Completely stunned, Shayne watched as Flynn stormed out and shouted, "Quick! Call an ambulance!"

WHITEY O'LEARY stepped out of the telephone booth and let out a sigh of deep concern. He'd tried to warn them, but was obviously too late. There'd been no answer.

"Any luck, Whitey?" Squint Mulligan asked.

"No," Whitey replied, as they both turned and looked down the block. The paddy wagon was parked outside the Quality Flour building. They had stood and watched as Flynn, Shayne, and the other cops had charged inside.

By a sheer stroke of luck, he and Squint had been just a few minutes late for the meeting with Nails. For him, that was like missing the Titanic and a sure date with destiny.

"Come on, let's get out of here," Whitey instructed. "This place'll be crawling with cops in no time."

"But what about the money?" Squint asked.

"Forget it," Whitey answered. "We'll just have to figure something else out."

WHEN Vicky Rose arrived at the crime scene, she was surprised to see the paddy wagon and two police cars driving away. She'd gotten there too late.

She'd had to drive all the way over from downtown. Had she and Denny gone back to Vicedomini's like he'd suggested, she'd have been a lot closer.

And just when she'd finally made the crime beat and really needed to prove that she she could cut it. Great work, Vick.

She looked around for Chester Lyons, but it appeared he'd already gone, too. Couldn't say she was disappointed.

The only vehicles still there were an ambulance and the coroner's car. Waiting by the ambulance was a white-haired Irish Priest, smoking a cigarette with a young Rookie cop.

So, she reasoned, there was one person later than her. Nails McCarthy. And he was getting ready for a one-way trip to the Morgue. The real one.

But the real icing on the cake was that *Terminal City Standard* reporters Charlie Hecht and Ben Gelbart had also beaten her there. No surprise, since every other reporter in town had done the same. Those two may have been second-rate, but they clearly had better contacts.

Naturally, they were the first ones to greet her. With all the smarm they could muster, of course.

"You're too late, Doll Face," Charlie heckled, while still managing to give her his usual once-over. "Missed the whole thing."

"Must've been out getting her hair done," Gelbart chuckled, throwing a quick elbow Charlie's way.

"So, any chance you mugs want to fill me in on what happened?" Vicky asked. She tried to sound sincere but was unable to mask the disdain in her voice. "Help a girl out?"

"Normally, we don't make it a habit of assisting the competition," Charlie began, checking her over once more. "But what kind of gentlemen would we be if we didn't help out a fair damsel in distress?"

His lascivious grin made her want to punch him right in the kisser. But that wouldn't have gotten her the information she needed.

"Would you?" she asked, smiling through clenched teeth as she opened her notebook.

Charlie straightened his tie, then gave her the scoop. "Detective Sergeant Michael Flynn, that's with two Ns, killed Nails McCarthy and even took a bullet himself!"

"Wait, Nails McCarthy is dead?" Vicky reacted with surprise. *Make that the third surprise in less than five minutes,* she thought. So, that's who was headed to the Morgue. All the flower shops in town were about to get really busy.

"Yeah," Gelbart added. "Detective Flynn's a true hero! City needs more cops like him."

"That's right," Charlie bragged. "We're on our way to the hospital right now to get an exclusive with Flynn. See ya there, Doll Face!"

They chuckled to themselves as they jumped in Charlie's car and drove off. Hats off to them.

Vicky stood there in shocked disbelief. Not just for barely missing out on a major scoop, but for what Nails' death meant for the city. With Whitey still on the lamb, there'd be nothing stopping Big Jack and the South Side mob from taking over now.

Vicky was about to follow the boys to the hospital, when she realized maybe that wasn't the best idea. Every other reporter in town had that angle covered. Instinct told her to stick around. And instinct was about to pay off in spades.

Not even five minutes had passed before the medics carried out Nails' body on a stretcher. He was covered in a sheet that was deeply stained with blood.

They were followed by a tall, clean-cut cop. She'd seen him around. Thought his name was Shayne, but she wasn't sure. Might have even read about him in the paper once before.

He'd already loosened his tie and took a big step back when they reached the ambulance. His hands were bloody and he didn't seem to notice. He seemed pretty frazzled by the whole situation.

Big guy like that? Surely this wasn't his first stiff. Now that would have been a *real* surprise.

But that was nothing compared to the biggest shock of all. In a night of surprises, this one took the triple crown.

The Priest threw away his smoke and knelt down to perform last rites.

He crossed himself and said a prayer, then reacted with a start.

After a moment of stunned silence, he cautiously lowered his head to the corpse's chest. Then he quickly straightened right back up.

"This man lives!"

READ THE NEXT EXCITING CHAPTER!

**A crusading reporter out to prove her worth.
A burgeoning hero in denial about his.**

When a Mob Boss is gunned down by police, Daily Crusader reporter Vicky Rose is the only one who suspects he was unarmed. Desperate to justify her promotion to the crime beat, her search for the truth leads her into a cesspool of corruption deeper than she ever imagined.

Brent Gregor, his existence as The Black Spectre still a deeply-held secret, only wants to use his newfound powers to win back what he has lost. And to take revenge on those who took it from him.

Both face unexpected consequences that could cost them their lives. And both have to decide if what they wanted was actually worth the price.

www.blackhoodpress.com

READ THE NEXT EXCITING CHAPTER!

A masked hero fights for his life. An ailing reporter faces uncertain death. Will either live until morning?

Following his failed attempt to kill Big Jack, Brent Gregor (aka The Black Spectre) lies near death in a Chinatown parish. Determined to locate the mysterious assassin, the Mob combs the blood-soaked streets to find him. His only hope of survival lies in the mercy of strangers.

Furious that she missed out on the story of a lifetime, Vicky is stunned to learn that her mysterious savior is actually real. Ignoring Editor Frank Matson's orders and her own failing health, she goes after the story with a vengeance. But to get the answers she so desperately needs, she will have to march straight into the lion's den. Alone.

www.blackhoodpress.com

About the Author

Roger Alford grew up on a steady diet of *Star Wars* and Jim Henson. After discovering old time radio and movie serials in college, he realized he'd been born in the wrong decade. His Internet videos, which include the popular mash-ups *The Twilight Zone: Planet of the Apes* and *Raiders of the Lost Ark: The Serial*, have been featured on ABC News, CNN, Inside Edition, plus multiple books and newspapers. When he's not plotting the latest adventures of The Black Spectre or brushing up on Mafia history, he's traveling the country and eating in great restaurants with his wife and family.

PINEAPPLE: 17-10-17-24-20-3 10-15-20-6-16 13-18-20-2 12-9-14 11-9-23-16 3-18-16-17 3-21 3-11-16 12-21-1

www.ingramcontent.com/pod-product-compliance
Lightning Source LLC
Chambersburg PA
CBHW032124170626
46808CB00006B/2099